Chemical Burns

Chemical Burns

Harry Carpenter & Timothy R. Baldwin

Midnight Destiny Publishing

Contents

Contents

Contents

"Dedicated to some police friends that cringed when I wrote certain things wrong. Thanks for correcting some, even though I'm stubborn and took creative liberties.
Also dedicated to my wife, who continues to put up with my crazy. I fear one day she will assume I am, in fact, a serial killer."

-Harry Carpenter

"Dedicated to my sister, who luckily doesn't fit the killer's MO for victims. Stay brunette!"

-Timothy R. Baldwin

Preface

Parkside, Michigan. A quaint town to raise any middle-class family. The reasonable school system and the growing economy of this once industrial-centric town make it the ideal place to settle. While every bustling metropolis has it's faults, Parkside seemed in short supply. That is, until recent events turned the town upside down.

Detective Sergeant Kurt Morgan had it all, and watched it slip through his fingertips. A lead position in a recently restructured homicide department, an adoring wife and two children; the perfect life. An overzealous Morgan, along with his partner, Detective Terry Coombs, persued a killer decades in the making. In the heat of the action, Detective Coombs was pronounced dead on the scene.

Devastated, Morgan tried to put away the pair of killers, aptly dubbed "The Crazed Lovers," by any means possible. Long nights and weekends away from home drove a wedge between him and his loving, and as understanding as possible wife Zahra. She and the two children became second fiddle to a workplace obsession. Soon after, Morgan began drinking heavily, a futile attempt to mask the pain of the real world. Following not far behind, Zahra filed for divorce.

Devastated and alone, Morgan attempts to get enough of his senses together to take on another great challenge: The Chemical Burn Killer. He has to solve this one. If not for his family, then for his late partner, Coombs.

◊◊◊◊

Jasper Marks was an up-and-coming reporter with a few blockbuster articles under his belt. He had a prosperous career, an adoring girlfriend named Becca, and a friendly rivalry with her best friend and fellow reporter, Patti Pruiet. Things were progressing very well for Jasper before the well ran dry. Article after article seemed to be the same boring drivel.

His editor-in-chief, Mr. Grayson, demanded more and more. He wanted the money shot, as it were. Articles about taxpayer complaints, animal adoptathons, and the local school teacher's latest good deed just didn't tickle his fancy anymore. He wanted something with zip. Grayson demanded to most of Jasper with the ultimatum of a lifetime: get the article I want, or get out of my sight.

With everything laid on the line by Grayson, Jasper is in desperate need of a miracle or something short of one. He needed something with the grit and grime that Grayson desired. Jasper Marks was not a man who was known for taking things lying down. He wanted to be the boots-on-ground reporter that people spoke of for generations to come, no matter what the cost.

{ 1 }

Chapter 1

The blood felt warm between my fingers as I recoiled my hand back from the body. A young girl, possibly twenty, thirty at best, lay partially dismembered in a suitcase. The killer made no effort to hide the body. For that matter, the bag looked like a mode of transporting the body across the room, as indicated by the scuff marks and apparent scrapes on the ground. Even through my gloved hands, I still felt disgusting.

"Detective Morgan, thank god you're here!" a voice cried out from behind me. It was one of the local boys I'd linked up with on a similar case. "What are your thoughts, sir?"

Christ, my thoughts? My thoughts were racing. I tried to map the scene in my mind as best as I could, attempting to recreate the killer's methodology as best I could. She struggled; that much was clear. Her left hand had been dissected, mangled beyond recognition. Her fingernails were plucked, likely in a violent fashion. Judging by the damage, this young lady was alive at the time. I'd tell this cop to check the feet for similar damage, but they were removed, likely somewhere else out there. Hopefully, they were still here, unless the killer took a trophy.

"You think it's the same guy?" the officer asked. "You know, the guy that chops his victims? Burns their fingerprints off?"

"I don't know, kid."

I reached out to the outstretched wrist. The victim's hands were balled into a fist, albeit gently. I used a pen to pull apart her hands. I was almost hoping she'd have a tuft of our killer's hair or a tear of fabric clutched in her palm. Her fingers, once pulled back, were caked in blood and what appeared to be dirt. I scraped a bit off to reveal what we already knew: her fingertips were burned off.

"Sir?" The officer asked. "Detective?"

"It's our man. It's the same sonofabitch," I said, letting her hand relax back into a gentle fist as the rigor mortis already began to set in.

What a way to go. Until the coroner and forensics arrive, I'd have to speculate whether or not she was alive when all of these unspeakable acts went down. In my gut, I think I had my answer. The mere thought of it made my mouth water in prep for vomit. This was someone's girlfriend. She was a daughter or a mother. This was a person simply tossed about like yesterday's plaything for the garbage. I stood to my feet.

"Detective Morgan, thank you for coming," a voice said from across the room. It was the police lieutenant, Lieutenant Weems. "Christ, another one?"

I began removing my gloves for disposal, being extra careful not to touch the outside of them. "It would seem so."

Weems rubbed the bridge of his nose. "That's the third one this month. Same MO?"

"Female. I'm guessing aged twenty to thirty based on what was left. Blonde hair strands remained on her scalp. The same chemical solvent used, far as I can tell."

"And the hands?"

"Fingernails plucked, as usual."

"Jesus H. Forensics is en route. I'll have an update once we have something more," Weems said. "Go home and get some rest. You've pushed harder than anyone, and lack of sleep will not do anyone justice."

LT's words bounced around in my exhausted brain, but he was right. I'd been up for damn near three days at this point, starting with Wednesday. The girl was found in the alleyway behind the abandoned theatre. That was the first this week. The kills always came in threes, and we just found our trio. I took one last look around the scene, taking it all in, observing all of the splatters of gore on the walls, the entrails that hung lazily from a metal bin. I knew the gruesome scene would be burned into my brain, much like the others. I took my leave, heading to my car.

I checked my phone once in the driver's seat. Two missed calls: one from my section chief and the other from my therapist. I should be more attentive to at least one of them, but fuck 'em. I'll check in with the chief tomorrow. The therapist would have to wait until I was damn good and ready to talk. For now, I needed to see my regular shrinks: Jack, Jameson, or Johnny. I set off down the road to my favorite haunt, just below my apartment.

The neon lights greeted me as I pulled up to the parking lot. The hum of cheap wiring buzzed at the front door, likely from the thirty-year-old Budweiser sign. I didn't care. Willy's was close, it was cheap, and it was all I needed to get through tonight. I sat at my usual barstool, signaling to the bartender. Without hesitation, Dan began pouring my usual Whiskey sour on the Rocks. They may as well call it The Morgan at this point. I swirled the glass before finishing the first in two swigs. Before the glass had hit the bar top, another was in its place. It indeed was a place where everyone knew your name.

Chapter 2

"Marks!" A gruff voice called out over the ticking of journalists huddled in cubicles as they pounded out their stories. My ears burned as I stood to see out over my cubicle wall.

The editor-in-chief, G. Greyson Griffin, stared out over the newsroom. His thick dark mustache seemed to dance over his upper lip as he chewed on a stogie. He pointed at me, then turned into his glass office.

"Good luck, Jasper," Patti Pruiet, the platinum blonde in the cubical next to mine, sang.

I gave her a glance, and she swiped the long bangs of her pixie cut to the side of her face.

I grinned. "Probably nothing. You know Griffin."

She rolled her eyes. "Do I ever."

"See you on the flipside," I said.

"If you survive," Patti said as she scooted her chair closer to her desk.

"Thanks for the vote of confidence."

I headed toward the office, keenly aware that everyone I passed seemed to hunker further down in their cubicles as if they needed to avoid becoming collateral damage to whatever Griffin had in store for me today.

I finished my internship with the Daily Sentry just over five years ago. At the time, I was the first new hire in nearly five years. Then, Patricia Saunders, or Patti as we affectionately called her, came along a year ago. Soon after, Griffin placed me in the position of senior reporter once the paper's most tenured journalist retired. Patti became the new kid and my mentee.

How does one describe Patti other than to say she was the whole package? Smart, sexy, athletic — every man's dream girl rolled into one person. She got a kick out of writing sensational pieces, ones that contained every bit of zest and fire to match her personality. She dated women who's spunk matched those of the articles she wrote. Each woman was a real firecracker, to say the least. To say Patti and I worked well together would be an understatement. Nonetheless, Patti was prepared to spread her wings and take the lead on the next scoop. While basking in the success of my trainee, I quickly realized what Griffin summonded me for.

I paused in my trek toward the editor's office. Above the water cooler, an inspirational poster of a mountain climber atop Mount Everest read, *"Achievement: It is hard to fail, but it is worse never to have tried to succeed."* One of the many Roosevelt quotes that resonated through time. It served a dual purpose: for some, the poster served as a taunt those whose writing had gone stale, while for others, the message spurred them on to strive for greatness. I was in the latter category.

The watercooler gossip suggested I'd impressed the other editors with a few good pieces in the past year. I'd nailed the scoop on the missing funds at the children's annual pageant, and I cracked open the mystery of the coffee shop notorious for serving stale donuts on the regular. Other write-ups consisted of assisting in the coverage of the mayor's ball or reporting on the town's latest gossip.

"Marks!" Griffin's voice called out again. I turned.

"What are you? A statue? A Mannequin? Time is money, my boy. Gargoyles don't get paid to stand around and stare at posters," Griffin said. "Now get in my office!"

I followed this time, not stopping until I stood in front of him, a stack of my old articles spread across his desk.

"What is this?" Griffin asked, holding up a familiar photograph of the coffee shop.

"It's one of my stories, sir," I said.

The paper rustled in Griffin's hand. "You're damn right it is!" Griffin fanned his hand over my work that littered his desk. "And you wrote all these since you were still wet behind the ears. Now, what've you got to say for yourself?"

"I can do better," I offered.

"What happened to the old bravado?" Griffin asked. "You used to write with gusto, pizzazz. Your writing had balls! Don't tell me that your little lady friend tucked those away in her purse and now keeps them under lock and key."

He was talking about Becca Luckner, my girlfriend of almost a year and Patti's former college roommate.

Griffin slapped me on the shoulder and roared with laughter. "I'm kidding with you. Don't take life so seriously."

He sat, then shuffled through some more papers. He held up one of my latest pieces with a humorless expression in his eyes. "But this, Marks, you must take seriously. Everything we do here at this paper should be serious."

I nodded.

He pointed at one of the drafts of my pieces. "This is ridiculous. Foot patties? Disgusting."

"But the story —"

He held up a hand. "No. This just won't do." He tore up the draft and tossed it to the floor. Then he leaned in and glared at me.

"Jasper Marks, you've been with the paper for almost five years. The other editors rooted for you as the lead investigative reporter. But I promoted you because I believed in you."

"I appreciate —"

Griffin held up a hand. "But your writing has lost some of its old bravadoes since your promotion. Does Severna Falls really have nothing happening? Or are you getting lazy?"

I sat. "On the contrary, sir. I'm working on something big."

"Something new, I hope. I'm tired of The Gazette getting the scoop on our local news before us."

"I promise you The Gazette will not have picked up on this story."

He sat back down and folded his arms. "Are you going to keep me in suspense, or are you pulling this out of your ass?"

"I'm working through the details."

He narrowed his eyes and grunted. "This better be good, Marks. Get me something by Monday."

I stood, keeping my poker face intact. "I will. Now, if you'll excuse me, I need to finish that story about the toe-jam patties."

Griffin howled. "That's the spirit! The sooner you get that out of the way, the sooner you'll get me something big. And, just so you know, you'll be reporting directly to me. No middleman, you got that?"

"Thank you, sir. I won't let you down."

I returned to my desk and sat with a sigh.

Patti popped out from her cubicle. "Tough old bird. What's he got you doing?"

"A big story," I said.

"Care to loop me in?"

I shook my head, leaned into my cubicle, and mumbled, "If only I was looped in."

"What's that?" Patti's muffled voice replied.

"I'll need to gather more evidence," I said with more gusto. "But I'll let you know when I'm ready."

"You better," Patti said. Then she returned to her work, and the rhythm of her keyboard lulled me into procrastination.

When I scanned through the blotters and social media outlets, I didn't know what I expected to find. Article after article, nothing proved helpful. Not a single hot tip from a tagged post on Twitter, despite my massive following of just over a thousand. While not bad for a reporter in a small-town paper, my girlfriend, Becca, harps on me that I need to get a more expansive presence and grow my social media networks. I didn't know what that meant, and I didn't know enough to feign knowledge or admit ignorance.

I returned to the story Griffin had ripped apart. It wasn't ground-breaking, and it certainly wouldn't make the first page, but it wasn't fluff either. A popular fast-food chain had disgruntled employees. Those employees decided to throw frozen beef patties on the floor and stomp on them with bare feet before frying them up and serving them to customers.

Griffin did have a point, though. I'd scraped the bottom of the barrel for that story. I'd get paid for two-thousand words, and the employees would be fired. Meanwhile, the fast-food chain would be held to a higher standard.

I needed something substantial. Griffin's voice rang in my ears: "You're an investigative reporter. Now, investigate!"

{ 3 }

Chapter 3

None of it made sense. Not one sliver of it. I stared at the open case files on this desk for hours. Each girl shared one similarity; they were all mutilated in the same way. The hair color, body shape, location; it all connected—until it didn't. I took a sip from my coffee, Irish style. as always. The Jack Daniels seemed to keep me grounded. Then again, Jack, Johnny, and Jim have been the only ones appearing to give half a shit about me in a long time. They're always there when I need them. This mutilating sicko was about to become another cold case for me.

Not since losing Terry Coombs to a senseless act of heroism have I felt right. It's been nagging at my brain ever since. The scene was so gruesome. I figured I was struggling with catching the Crazed Lovers, undoubtedly named because this man and wife duo were traveling around and murdering people. Coombs and I worked our asses off to track them down. Christ, we went so far as to call in all hands-on deck down in Arkansas to fan out the mid-west for these assholes. The bodies. The way some of those people died. It was all so...inhuman. One was decapitated via a properly placed coat hook and some body-weight. Some other choked on a spoon. I guess it was too much for Coombs.

The day I went over to his house is a day I won't ever forget. His wife had just returned from Pilates or something to find he'd blown himself to kingdom come all over the China cabinet with his service weapon. I'd been involved with the Crazed Lovers case for damn near two decades; Coombs only for about a quarter of that. It was enough to turn you, that's for damn sure. This mutilating son of a bitch, however, he's different. Something about him. I rubbed my temples feverishly in frustration.

"Long shift there, Detective Morgan?" a voice called out behind me.

"Yeah, this damn mangler fella with the chemicals. I can't figure him," I said, looking back to see one of the rookie cops eyeballing my case file.

I'd been attached to work with the local PD ever since these crimes became serial. They stayed outta my way, I stayed outta theirs. We shared information and thoughts, and that's as far as the relationship went.

"No offense, and I don't mean this the wrong way and with due respect for the dead and all, but she's got a shit dye job."

I looked back at the assortment of victim photos splayed around my desk.

"That one. The one that's clearly a blonde masquerading as a brunette. It's an easy call. Must have been a few weeks since the coloring."

I grabbed the dark-haired girl's photo and took a closer look. He was right: she's a blonde. I scrambled through the other victim photos to check the rest.

"Aw, these girls dyed their hair; just look at 'em!" the rookie laughed. "Anyway, I'll leave you to it. Don't stay up too late."

The rookie finally left me alone with my thoughts for a moment. As much as I didn't want to be bothered, he had a point. As a matter of fact, he had a big fucking point. They all dyed their hair! The ones who weren't sporting the natural golden locks altered their look, but he knew. The killer fucking knew! *How could I miss that?* I took a final swig of my coffee to finish the cup before hurling the empty Styrofoam into my bin.

I quickly grabbed up my jacket and wiped my mouth off. I tossed in several Tic-Tacs from my jacket pocket before making my way outside in the event I ran into someone of importance just to not smell like booze. I needed some air and some time to think. Pieces were starting to click, and I needed to wrap my head around them. Once I was outside the department, I lit up a fresh cigarette. I suppose technically this was the first one of the day, in a manner of speaking. The streetlights were still lit as the sun broke through the city streets ever slightly. People were on the move trying to begin their commute to work, and here I was on day two of a nearly forty-hour binger. I took several drags before putting out the cigarette under my boot. My ex-wife hated when I smoked.

I made my way back to my workspace, gathered up my things into my shoulder bag, and headed out of the precinct. I hated taking my work home, but it happened more often than not. I needed to get some sleep. I missed such a minutiae detail; how the hell else can I be sure I won't miss anything like that again? I fumbled for the keys in my left pocket for a moment, pressing the alarm on the car. The green Ford Focus lit up like Christmas as I pressed the key. I made my way home as fast as I could.

Once in the apartment, I shuffled through broken and empty bottles and cans to the one piece of furniture I owned: a broken-down grey sofa bed that didn't pull out anymore. I took a pit stop in the kitchen to retrieve one or two Budweisers from the fridge before slogging over to the couch, collapsing in a heap of alcohol and exhaustion. The images of the girls kept flashing through my mind. They weren't any more than a hundred pounds soaking wet. They were outmatched, outgunned, and outwitted by some asshat who liked to pick on the innocent and weak. But why burn them up? Why destroy them? I closed my eyes, letting my brain slowly digest those questions before drifting off into sleep.

{ 4 }

Chapter 4

The following day, the ringing of the telephone jolted me awake. After fumbling with the phone and myself, my father's voice greeted me on the other end.

"Jasper, you should've been down here fifteen minutes ago. I already ordered."

"I'll be there in five," I said and hung up the phone. I called out, "Becca, you didn't wake me!"

An empty apartment returned my complaint with silence. I'd overslept and, rather than waking me, Becca had gone off to work.

After a quick piss and a splash of water on my face, I donned my oxford shirt and jeans hanging on the back of the door. Then I slipped on some shoes and speed-walked the two blocks to the diner. I spotted my father sitting at the usual corner window booth as I approached the restaurant.

With a chime, the door opened to waitresses doing their usual dance between tables as they took orders and refilled coffee mugs for the patrons. My father wore earbuds, and he kept a wary eye on the restaurant activity. I knew his routine, and he wasn't listening to music. No, he had the dial turned to a different channel.

I sat across from him and waited. He put down his paper and jotted down a few notes on a legal pad he kept by his side. He put his pen down when he'd finished writing, then he looked at me as if noticing my arrival for the first time. Taking out his earbuds, he grinned.

"What's the news, pop?" I asked.

He took a sip of coffee, and I flipped my mug over.

"The usual," my father said. "Shooting down on West Avenue. Then some kids tagging freight trains on the south side of town."

Ever the hobbyist, my father took up listening to the police scanners years ago. When I was a kid, the thing was permanently set up in his woodshop where he'd memorize the ten codes while working on a bench or a hide-away chest. After demanding a tool, he'd tell me what the codes meant. I'd soaked up the knowledge while I handed him a wrench or a Phillips-head screwdriver. Maybe that's what got me into journalism with an emphasis on crime. That, and I was too scrawny for police work.

The waitress came to our table and filled my mug as I confirmed my usual order of hashbrowns, scrapple, and two buttermilk pancakes. As she walked away, my father asked, "How's work?"

I took a sip of coffee. "Nothing award-winning as of late," I told Dad about the fast-food story, and his eyes lit up.

"You mean to tell me I've been going there every Thursday for the last ten years, and that's what they did with their burgers?"

"Good thing you always get the fish fillet," I said.

He waved my comment away. "But have you latched onto your next big story?"

I picked at the place-mat paper menu. Then I told my father about Griffin's demand for a new story idea by Monday.

My father grunted. "Shouldn't be too hard to manage." Then he flipped through the legal pad. After several pages, he paused and studied everything for a moment.

"What is it?" I asked.

He tore the page out, folded it twice, then slid the paper toward me, hiding it beneath his palm. I reached for the paper when he lifted his hand.

"Save it for later," my father instructed.

"What is it?"

He nodded, and I looked to my left. The waitress came with two hot plates. I stuffed the paper into my breast pocket as the waitress left.

"Something's happening across the lake," my father began.

I restrained my temptation to read the slip of paper until our conversation concluded.

"Dig in," my father said, shoveling scrambled eggs onto his fork.

Very little was spoken throughout the meal, short of the occasional complements to the chef. It seemd my father was jumping through hoops to not discuss the contents of the paper in my shirt pocket. I also knew better than to press him for details. These would come later. Besides, I landed a few of my stories due to my father's many tips from the police scanner. Whatever new information he'd given me could wait.

For now, though, my father and I ate our breakfast in silence.

{ 5 }

Chapter 5

The phone nearly vibrated off the table to the floor before I had time to reach for it. I fumbled, half-drunk, knocking bottles of beer and Jack all over.

"Keep your shirt on; I'm trying!" I said, lifting my head to see the phone angrily buzzing.

I swiped my thumb across the green call accept button and aggressively cleared my throat. "He—hello? This is Morgan."

I wiped a trickle of saliva that dangled from my cheek with the back of my hand before the caller spoke up, sucking in the remainder using the corner of my lip.

"You're not going to believe this one," the voice said.

"Try me."

"It's another one. Another girl, sir."

I sat up quickly. The entire room gently pivoted with me as my eyes adjusted to my new positioning. The alcohol sloshed around in my body as I jerked to my feet with the following statement.

"It's worse this time. She's, well, you'd better get down here," the voice said shakily.

"Get your shit together, officer. I'll be there. Text me the address," I said, rubbing my eyes as I stood to make for the fridge.

"Absolutely," there was a slight pause. "And, sent! I'll be here. See you shortly."

"Yeah, yeah," I replied as I hung up the phone.

I prepared my usual Alka-Seltzer and Gatorade combo to bring me back to Earth. I slammed that as I prepared the shower to wash the booze from my pores as best as possible. Allowing the hot water to steam the room before entering, the scalding temperature was more than plenty to jolt me out of any booze-induced haze I found myself in. After I washed, I quickly grabbed my cleanest set of clothing before moving to the door. I nearly forgot my gun and badge on the side table before shutting the door behind me.

Detective work had not been easy. I had a lot of ups and downs. I've reunited many families while explaining some semblance of closure to others. It was a hard job. Nearly two decades into this, it never seems to wane in difficulty. Pulling up to each crime scene felt new, yet, a repeat of days past. Eventually, the world began to look darker and grimmer with each passing second. I wanted nothing more than to put a bullet into every asshole who made this world a terrible place, but justice needed to run its course. This crime scene was no different as I parked outside of farm property, several miles outside of town.

"Detective Morgan, glad you could get here in time," a voice greeted me from beyond my headlights. "It's bad, sir. Real bad."

I flipped off the headlights and killed the engine. It was my lead forensics expert, Felicity. She and Dwayne were my go-to crew when I wanted to know the real dirt, so to speak. I stepped out of the vehicle and drew a cigarette from my jacket pocket. The cool air chilled my hands as I sparked my lighter.

"Is it more of the same?" I asked, taking a drag of my menthol cancer stick.

"I wish...wait, that came out wrong. Let's talk to D and have him give you what he's collected so far. Coffee?" Felicity asked as she pointed to the portable carafe from the local donut shop down the road.

I accepted and met Dwayne near the well-lit canopy which contained the mobile work center. I poured myself a cup of coffee as

Dwayne hurried over with a folder and notepad. He was your traditional Nervous Nelly of an analyst, but he was damn good at his job. I'd pegged him as mid-thirties, but Dwayne still seemed like a pup to me. He and Felicity were a dynamic duo when it came to shit like this. Felicity had the eye and the mind for finding the craziest details, and Dwayne worked his magic of making sense of it all. He'd make a hell of a detective if he went that path.

"So, here's what we know, sir," Dwayne started. "The level of dismemberment is wilder this go. We're determining what chemical compound was used to dissolve the bone, but there was enough to identify the VIC."

I took a long, strong sip of my coffee before replying. "What do you mean "enough left?""

Dwayne motioned for me to follow him to the right-most side of the building. He seemed eager to show off his latest find, as if proud of it in a sick way. Some in the industry live for this shit, and there are others who do this shit to live. I sat on the fence myself. There was a time when I was passionate about it. Perhaps not as much as Dwayne, but I had some spunk.

"She's, well, yeah. Over here," Dwayne said, motioning for a fellow officer to shine a light on a pile of debris on the floor near a few aluminum trashcans.

I watched as the flashlight beamed onto the pile. There was a trail of blood that could have filled a milk jug. It wasn't dry—too thick for that. The officer tilted his light to follow the path, leading to an area riddled with evidence markers and investigators. I felt it best to silently observe the trail.

"Jesus Christ," Felicity muttered while holding the crook of her arm over her mouth and nose.

In a pile of broken rock and sand sat a single hand, missing one finger. The index, to be exact. Most killers took trophies from the scene, so this wasn't uncommon. A body part was far from unheard of. Hell,

Ed Gein used to have boxes of vaginas in his linen closet. The guy was a freak. We were dealing with someone that might give ol' Eddie a run for his money.

"Check this out," Dwayne began. "We looked closely at the hand. The fingertips, if you can tell from over there, are missing. They're just burned off."

"Like the Men in Black?" Felicity quipped.

"Basically. We managed to get the word back to HQ, and we think we know who this is. Missing persons reported her about two weeks ago. She didn't show up for work, didn't come home, and nobody had seen her."

"We'll know more when the lab gets back with results," Felicity said, still working hard to not gag at the grotesque sight before her.

"Are we just testing what's left of the hand? That's gonna be a bit rough considering how much has been muddled with chemicals and additives," I queried.

Dwayne pointed toward a giant steel drum barrel at the far end of the building corner. It was just out of sight, yet our guys were already probing it.

"And that is?" I asked.

"Hair was found stuck to the barrel. And not just hair. About a third of her scalp with the brown hair still attached!" Dwayne exclaimed.

Felicity dry heaved slightly as she turned away. As a forensic investigator, I'm sure she's seen plenty, but even I felt this was a bit extreme.

"Wait, you said brunette?" I asked.

"Correct."

"Well, that fucks things up just a bit, doesn't it?" I said out gruffly. "Our guy was going after the blondes, so we assumed his M.O. Now we're back to the goddamn drawing board again."

I rubbed my temples in frustration. The sun began to come up over the horizon.

"Christ, I got my kids today," I said aloud.

"What was that?" Felicity asked.

"I got visitation with my kids today. Zahra is going to flip if I cancel again," I said, checking my cellphone.

"Go take care of that. I'll get everything on your desk this afternoon. Davey and Alisa need you more. Can't bail on them again!" Felicity jested.

I gave a slightly offended expression but agreed with that statement. I've let work come between myself and the kids all too often. It'd be a matter of time before they give up on me as Zahra did.

"Call or text me the second something comes through, ok?" I said as I walked toward the mobile work center to toss this coffee cup.

As I tossed my cup in the garbage, I looked at the donuts as one quick means of sustenance before seeing the kiddos. My stomach flopped a bit at the thought of eating. I decided I'd save myself for lunch with Davey and Alisa. I headed to my car and prepared to hit the apartment for a quick shower before my visit today. I looked and felt like hammered shit.

Chapter 6

The Daily Sentry had many benefits to one employed in its ranks. For me, it was the flexibility of hours. As an investigative reporter, I could come and go as I pleased. Though, I had ridden the clout of a handful of successful and sensational stories. I knew my rep points were wearing thin, especially when I arrived in the middle of a staff meeting.

Griffin let his disapproval known as he tracked my movements, glaring at me while he chewed the tip of a cigar. Then he spat out a piece of tobacco when I sank in beside Patti. A few pairs of eyes gave me the once over before returning their attention to Griffin.

"Most of you know this already, but I'm going to say it anyway," Griffin said. "Our competitor, The Gazette, is beating us to stories."

A bone-thin geek in a baggy suit spoke up. "But, sir, they've got twice the staff, and their stories are mostly —"

"Fluff? Hogwash? Gibberish?" Griffin sputtered. "Don't I know it!"

"That's not what I was...," The geek's voice trailed off. Then he took a seat as Griffin railroaded the man's commentary.

"All of you know what it takes. That's why we hired you. For your go-getter attitudes. Do you remember when you were hungry? I do. But lately, our readership and rankings have been sinking. We need to do something about that. Marks can't be the only one with a good story to tell."

I sank into my chair in a failed attempt to disappear.

"What've you got for us, Marks?" Griffin asked.

I stood, and all eyes — hostile and mildly amused — were glued to me. I stuffed my hand in my pocket and played with the slip of paper my father had given me. Then I prayed a silent Hail Mary and cleared my throat.

"I'm working on something big," I said, and I swear I heard at least a half dozen gasps mingled with murmurs. Before Griffin could pull it out of me, I added, "It's still in its infancy, but I'll shoot something to you by the end of the day."

Griffin grinned and pinched the cigar in his mouth. His exuberance didn't last long when he shifted his gaze onto a senior staffer in short sleeves. The staffer managed to choke out an elevator pitch for a story on the local high school sports. His synopsis was barely finished when Griffin moved on to another staffer. Soon the weekly inquisition wrapped up, leaving several journalists speechless as they rethought their career decisions. I, on the other hand, returned to my cubicle.

As soon as I sat, Patti wasted no time scooting over to me. "What've you got, Jasper? You know I could use a good story."

I didn't know myself, so I was glad for the sudden ringing of my phone. "Excuse me. I'm following up on a lead."

I huddled myself into the cubicle as deep as I could and picked up the cell on the fourth ring.

"Hey, Jasper," Becca's voice seemed to sing. "I'm sorry I had to dip out early this morning, but work called in need of coverage."

She worked at an upscale jeweler and despite the hours, she still managed to hit the gym and keep herself looking sexy as hell.

"It's no problem," I said. I glanced around and lowered my voice. "We're still on for tonight, yeah?"

"Are you still getting out on time?" Patti asked.

"Babe, you know I will."

"You better," she said. "I'm gonna wear that dress you like."

"Eight o'clock," I said. "I love you."

"I love you, too," Becca said. "I can't wait for this surprise you've got for me."

We ended the call, and I realized I'd gained an audience.

"The great Jasper Marks at work," Patti said. "You better be glad no one else noticed. I won't tell if you loop me in on your big story."

"Fine," I said, turning quickly away, pulling out the slip of paper, and unfolding it. Three words were scribbled on it: *women. mutilated. murder.* Beneath these three words, my father had scrawled *Parkside, Michigan.*

I grabbed my computer and fired it up. At first, my search came up with some references to a NY Times bestseller. But by the third page, my search turned out a handful of police blotters, most dated years back in other towns. Then I came to one as recent as yesterday. It was vaguely written.

Body of Third Victim Found. Hands Missing. Police Asking For Leads.

The body of a young woman was found in the 300 block of Lakeland Drive. While police are asking citizens for any information that may help catch the perpetrator, they are too early in their investigation to connect these otherwise random strings of bodies to the work of one killer. Citizens are asked, however, to be wary.

I scoffed. Who did the cops think they were kidding?

Another search, and I found a handful of precincts that would likely be involved in this investigation. But one after another, I found myself stonewalled with the same line about an active investigation. Then I tried a different approach.

"Patti, oh Patti," I sang as I wheeled my chair close to the cubicle wall we shared.

Patti answered with an abrupt, "Whaddya want?"

"I've got a favor to ask of you."

"Does it come with the partnership on the story?"

"You betcha," I said.

I filled her in on what I'd found. Then I hit her with the favor. "Find out who the lead investigator is, and we'll be co-authoring this piece."

She disappeared behind her cubicle, and I returned to the story about the unsanitary practice of flattening beef patties with bare feet. I resolved several editorial remarks, proofread the piece again, then sent it off for tomorrow morning's paper. While it wasn't my best writing, I knew it was better than ninety percent of the news churned out by the Sentry.

Then I got to work on an op-ed piece as a follow-up on a previous work-up I did about a disbarred attorney and her financial scandal. Like the other small-town players in this town, she was well-connected. Some would even go so far as to say she was one of the *good old boys*, those wheelers and dealers who everyone knows are sketchy, but no one has the guts to point the finger or the wherewithal to come up with any compelling or substantial evidence against them.

By the end of the day, an enthused Patti came to me. "His name's Morgan. He's practically a ghost, and he's a hard-ass."

I raised an eyebrow. "Did you speak to him? This Morgan guy?"

Patti laughed. "Hardly. I got a hold of the secretary to a captain at one of the precincts. She wouldn't divulge anything about the case, but she did advise us to stay out of the guy's way."

I shrugged. "So, we fly under the radar and take extra precautions not to be noticed."

"And do everything by the books," Patti said. "We don't want to make an enemy out of this guy."

"That still leaves us with little more than what we already have. It's not nearly enough to get a story to Griffin."

Patti had a twinkle in her eye. "I'm definitely in, right?"

"Does the moon rise over Miami?"

Patti laughed. "I also have a source, a rookie cop, who's seen some things."

"How's he related to you?" I asked.

"The boyfriend of a cousin," Patti said. "She says he's willing to talk to us."

"What's his angle?" I urged.

"Well, it's not money," Patti said. "Maybe he doesn't know any better."

"Or maybe he's looking for his fifteen minutes of fame," I said. "Does he know we'll keep him anonymous?"

"He knows, but he'll only talk to the lead investigator on the story. That'll be you. Here." She handed me a slip of paper. "Call him after your little date tonight."

Patti and I returned to our desks. It was already five minutes to Griffin's arbitrary daily deadline for new work. However, he'd be pleased to find we'd made headway on what I hoped to be a big scoop. I tapped out two hundred words, pitching Patti as my co-author on this investigation. Griffin, I was sure, would eat this story up, especially since murder and mutilation were involved. He got off on that stuff.

{ 7 }

Chapter 7

I drove through the city traffic with about a billion thoughts mulling about in my brain. Who the hell was this guy? Is he targeting an age? Is it their looks? It isn't hair color, that's for sure. The possibilities bounced around to the point of making me dizzy. That could also have been the last of the Jack coursing through my bloodstream. I figured I should hit the gas station for a Red Bull on the way to Zahra's home. My old home. The city's industrial zone, Bridgeview Terrace, was an oasis just outside of Parkside. At least, it used to be. Now it was a painful reminder of how much of a fuck up I was.

I was on autopilot as I continued my drive, fueled by sugar, caffeine, and jet fuel, whatever the hell they put in these drinks. Trees and cars passed by, my brain barely making a note of anything other than moving the vehicle forward. My radio was off, which was unusual for me. Most anyone who had been in my car knew I was notorious for blasting The Talking Heads. Surrealist music was always my escape, and their music really was something else. I considered firing up my "Remain in Light" album but figured I was only a few blocks away from the house, and it best not to waste my energy on car karaoke.

The house looked quiet. Hell, the whole street looked quiet for eight in the morning. I was about an hour early for my time with the kids, but Zahra would understand. She always did. I parked on the street. Any time I've been to the house since the divorce, I've felt

{ 25 }

like the driveway was a privilege, even though I still contribute to the mortgage. I popped a handful of Tic-Tacs into my mouth, smoothed my hair down, and exited the car for the front door. I looked like hammered shit that had been hit by a semi-truck.

I had barely raised a finger to press the doorbell before Zahra thrust open the door with a shriek. I'm sure I let out a small yelp, but I couldn't tell through my exhaustion. She dropped the garbage bag from her left hand and clutched her chest in her adrenaline-fueled startle.

"Christ, you scared me!" Zahra breathed, still trying to compose herself.

I rubbed the back of my head in embarrassment.

"Sorry about that. I'm a little early. Let me help you with that," I said, reaching down for the garbage bag.

"No, I got—"

"Here to help," I said, cutting her off as I clutched the bag's handles.

We calmly walked out to the garbage cans around the corner, not saying anything. Frankly, I felt too exhausted to compose a quality conversation. As I tossed the garbage into the can, I felt Zahra grab my bicep.

"How is the case?"

"The what?"

"I know that look, Kurt. You're on a case. I wasn't married to you as long as I was without knowing how you looked after a sleepless night on the job."

"Is it that obvious?" I sheepishly asked.

"Come inside. Let me get you a coffee," Zahra urged as she headed toward the front door.

The inside of the house hadn't changed much at all. The furniture hadn't been rearranged since I moved out. The walls were still the same color. The only difference I could see was a new painting hung in the hallway. Zahra was always collecting impressionist art. This looked like some knock-off Monet or something.

"Kids are in the den watching their movie again," Zahra said, motioning toward the den as if I didn't know where it was.

"Frozen again?" I asked.

"Frozen. Again."

Zahra poured two large mugs of coffee as she rolled her eyes at the thought of watching that film for the hundredth time this week. She sat down at the breakfast bar nook, and I followed suit. I didn't know that I needed a coffee, but she pushed a mug in my direction regardless. I figured it would be rude not to accept.

"Anything you can tell me?" Zahra asked.

She hated my work. It's not that she didn't think it was a good job or that I wasn't doing good for the world. She despised the fact I was always away, and the job essentially consumed me. The fact that she was asking about it blew me out of the water.

"Sure, if you want. We think we have a serial killer on our hands."

Zahra spat her coffee back into her mug. "A what?"

"We're not sure yet. The guys are confident it's the same guy. I was up most of the night at a scene near a warehouse. The poor girl didn't stand a chance. The sicko went too far."

Zahra leaned in, interested in the details. "How so?" She quickly glanced around for the kids, knowing they were being serenaded by Josh Gad right now and couldn't be bothered to trouble us.

"Well, the short of it? This guy has been mutilating bodies. We thought he took a trophy from the last one but found it on the scene."

"A trophy?" Zahra quizzed as she took a small sip from her mug.

"A finger."

I watched her eyes widen in disbelief. "In this city?"

"Unfortunately. It's been tearing me up. Seeing the kids would likely give me a good break from the chaos I just walked away from."

Zahra nodded, and I stepped away toward the den. I was greeted by a blast from the Disney film almost immediately, followed by my two children singing offkey with the movie.

"Daddy!" my daughter exclaimed as she jumped off the couch.

"Hey, Muffin! You're getting big!" I said, lifting her into the air just slightly over my head.

"What's going on, champ?" I asked my son, who barely looked my way.

A half-wave was given to me, as Davey never broke his eye contact with the television. He was hit hardest by the divorce. At thirteen, he was at that sweet age to already start to hate his parents, and I just gave him a reason to. Alisa was more welcoming. Or was it naive? Either way, having at least one of the kids pulling for me meant something. Zahra joined us and sat on the chaise in the corner of the room. I got that for her on our seventh anniversary, and honestly, it was the best investment I made. I don't think I've seen her enjoy anything else as much.

"I'm done after this one, by the way," I said out loud over the movie.

Zahra just nodded and looked back into her mug. I've said this several times before. I vowed to retire after my last big case, which went cold. I wore myself down back then. This guy was some cross-country wacko and did some dirty deeds nearby. I worked with the FBI on the case, and everything just went dead in '05. No trail, no clues. The last we heard of the guy, he left a dozen or so copies of a recording of his confession, if you will. No prints. No hair. He, or she, was good. That was the problem. We had reports of this guy being a female too, and vice versa. Other rumors pegged it as a couple. The news called them the Crazed Lovers. Hard to track when all we had were speculative eyewitnesses. He petered out as the Zodiac Killer did. Just cold.

"I'm serious!" I said with more tenacity this time.

"Daddy, let's watch the movie!" Alisa said, as she clutched her plush snowman in her arms.

I glanced over at Zahra briefly.

"We'll talk more about this later," she said as she curled up in her chair.

I'd be lost halfway through if I hadn't been subjected to this film more than a few dozen times. Some guy talking to his moose while a frigid bitch sings about wanting to be left alone on a mountain. My cartoons used to be simple. These things were so complex and layered that I can't follow them. Thankfully my kids ensure I watch them enough to get the gist.

My phone began to buzz in my jacket pocket. I looked at Zahra, who had just turned back to the television. I quickly jolted to my feet and moved toward the kitchen, answering my phone.

"Morgan here."

"Morgan? You're not going to believe this. We just got back some of the lab work, and this is a game-changer. We may have found a piece of the puzzle. Can you head down as soon as you can?" Felicity said on the other end of the phone.

"Sure. Give me a bit, and I'll be there," I replied.

She hung up without a moment's notice. The perks of "strictly business, no formalities or pleasantries."

"You have to go, don't you?" Zahra asked from behind me.

Slowly, I put my phone away as I turned around. "Yeah. Break in the case. I need to be there, as I'm the lead detective on the case."

"I get it. Do you want to just slip away, or should I let the kids know?"

"Slip away. I don't want to break the loop of the movie." I said reluctantly.

"They'll be pretty pissed when the credits roll, you know."

I gave a slightly displeased smirk before I started for the door. I needed to be at the station and couldn't afford a huge wave of good-byes with the kids. Once we had our pow-wow with the gang, I can probably come back and hang out. I have to know if she lets it go. Spoiler alert: she does. I fumbled for my car keys as I grabbed the doorknob.

"You're leaving us?" Alisa asked from my side.

She was like a damn ninja. She could be on my leg in seconds. I've had dogs that weren't as alert and sneaky in my past. Cats, too, for that matter.

"Honey, I have to go back to work. I promise, once I'm done, we'll watch any movie you want for as long as you want."

"Ok. You promised," Alisa said as she looked at her mother. "You heard he promised!"

She pointed an aggressive finger at me as she dramatically backed up toward the den.

"You promised," Zahra joked as she saw me to the end of the street.

"I'll call you if I can come back this way," I said, starting the engine. "I think they'd like that."

I smiled and adjusted my sun visor as I pulled off toward the precinct, heart heavy knowing that I likely would not be back to finish that movie.

{ 8 }

Chapter 8

Becca sat across from me at La Rosa Cafe, one of the town's premier Italian restaurants, which isn't saying much. While the town has more than one light, there isn't a whole lot to do. Becca wore a black dress with a low-cut V-neck top. Her shoulder-length brown hair was done up in curls with blonde highlights. While she was preoccupied with primping her hair so that I might take notice, I was preoccupied with thoughts of calling this nameless rookie cop and receiving confirmation from Griffin for the story.

When I still didn't comment on Becca's new hairdo, she frowned, then popped the evening's proverbial cherry and forced a smile. "You won't believe who came into the store today."

The phone in the inside pocket of my jacket buzzed. I reached for it. "Did the mayor come in again?"

Becca caught the movement of my hand, and her smile faded. "Jasper. What have I been telling you for the last three months? Seriously, I sometimes think you're a little too preoccupied with work."

I ignored the second notification on my phone and reached for the breadstick arranged in a basket on the table between us.

"I'm sorry," I said, then focused on Becca this time. I took in her perfume, which smelled of lilacs, and the vibrant lipstick she wore. "Griffin's given me an ultimatum."

She reached across the table and took my hand. "Jas. You know I'm your biggest supporter. Talk to me."

I sighed. "I finished that burger story."

She took her hand away and rolled her eyes. "The worst story you've been assigned but go on."

I broke off a piece of bread and chewed it contemplatively before continuing. "I sent Griffin two hundred words before heading out today. Way before I promised, and if I can't deliver the story, then it's back to fluff pieces, or worse."

Plates of salad arrived as a momentary distraction. The server offered freshly grated cheese and then served a helping on each of our dishes. When the server left, Becca picked up on the conversation, and she doused her salad with dressing.

"So, what's your story idea? Pitch it to me."

I tightened my lips, unsure she wanted to hear what my father and I uncovered. I went for it anyway. "Dad dropped me a tip this morning. When I got into the office, I found a few related cold cases, then a police blotter warning everyone to stay wary. This might lead to something big. But it's too soon to tell."

She nodded. "I get it. You don't want to let it out of the bag yet."

"Right," I lie, knowing she would disapprove of Patti working with me. "You were telling me about work."

She took a bite of her salad and chased it down with a sip of wine. "Big break today. You remember the football player, Trey Lewis."

"Didn't he just sign with the Seahawks?"

"Sure. But the point is Trey's been coming in for months now, checking out the same necklace."

I nodded. "The one with the signature floating diamond solitaire pendant."

Her eyes lit up. "So, you have been listening. Good. Well. Trey bought it today. You won't believe it. He dropped twenty-five grand all at once, and all that commission goes to me."

I raised my glass for a toast. As our glasses clinked, I reminded myself of the lesson in perseverance. "Wasn't that two years of a client relationship you were building?"

"Three, actually. And, on top of that," Becca paused for dramatic effect. "I'm pretty sure I'll be put in for top sales associate for the month, which means —"

"Another promotion," I finished her sentence and lifted my glass again. Becca's eyes sparkled, and we toasted to her success again.

Becca put the glass down and reached across the table. "What about you, though? You had a ring of great stories. Some even won awards. Do you think this new one can put you back on top?"

"That's what I'm hoping for. Griffin still has to approve this thing, though."

She nodded, then took another bite of her salad and chewed thoughtfully. "That's all great. Can you spare me any of the details?"

I shifted in my seat. Though I wanted to, I knew she wouldn't be able to keep a secret. Not with her co-workers at the jewelry store, a gossip mill if I'd ever seen one, and that's not even including the clients.

"Fine," Becca said. She picked up her napkin from her lap and wiped her mouth. Then she carefully folded it and laid it down on the table. "If you'll excuse me."

I watched as she made her way to the bathroom. When she'd disappeared, the bulge of my phone in the front pocket of my blazer seemed heavier, urging me to check my email. I slipped the phone out and opened my email. Of the multiple emails, one from Griffin was marked urgent. I opened it.

Marks. I checked out your lead. You've got two days to get me a preliminary report. Make it groundbreaking, sensational, and astonishing.

I closed my email and began to thumb out some ideas.

"Amazing!" Becca's voice broke my concentration. I looked up to see a spread set out before us.

"Radiant!" I add, taking in the blush of Becca's cheeks and her scowl.

Becca narrowed her eyes. "I was talking about your obsession with the phone. Seriously, how long has the food been here?"

"Not too long after you left."

"And how long ago was that?" she asked.

"Not long," I said, but she'd trapped me. "Listen, Griffin approved the story. I was just jotting down some ideas and got sidetracked."

She sighed. "We really need to get away from all of this. Just the two of us. Do you think you can do that?"

"Soon," I told her but kept out my hopes of traveling for work should the lead pay off.

Chapter 9

The station was buzzing with criminals, processing, computers, and phones. Officers rushed from end to end, while the fluorescent lights half-blinded me; we had such aggressive lighting in this station. Uniforms and plainclothes pushed past each other, rushing to their destinations without question. I slowly sauntered my way to the conference room. It was supposed to be a war or debriefing room, converted into a gentle conference room with a projector, fancy chairs, and a long table. It was more like a board meeting than anything. A change our chief wanted to make.

Before anyone could snag me, I bolted over to the coffee machine to grab a bit of energy before whatever mind-blowing, case-closing evidence we stumbled upon. I topped off a styrofoam cup and made my way to my desk to grab a little extra to toss into the cup. In my bottom drawer, I kept photos of my ex-wife, two spent bullets, and a bottle of gin. I fumbled past the picture of Zahra, hearing the bottle clank against the back of the drawer. I fondled the top for a moment, hesitating.

"Morgan! You're here!" Felicity said with excitement.

She was always a bright ray of sunshine. It didn't matter what she saw, how bad the scene was, or how disgusting the perp was. She always radiated happiness and hope.

"I just got in. I'll be with you guys in a moment."

I let go of the bottle, closing the drawer slowly, looking once more at the photo of Zahra and me. It was from our tenth anniversary and I looked stupid, as always. Things were simpler then. That photo was taken a few months before I got into the Crosstown Killer, the Killer Couple, or whatever the media wanted to call the guy or gal. I personally thought the Crazed Lovers was the better of the names. That case ate me up inside. It was half the reason for the bottle in my desk drawer — the other half were the bullets. They were removed from the abdomen of my partner, Cooms. That was before I was a detective, back when I was a beat cop working the streets. I decided it was high time to see what the fuss was about and made my way to the war room.

The conference room, rather, our war room, was adorned with photos of officers who retired, were killed in action, or earned meritorious marks for great deeds. Cooms' photograph was hung just next to the American flag on the far wall. I sat on the far-left side of the room, most distant from his memorial. Several officers filled the room, including a few other detectives and our forensics team, with our captain sitting just off to the side, arms crossed. He was a cold man. I should know; I played golf with him. He's maintained that same expression even when he's well under par.

"Ok, so we did some digging at this latest scene. We managed to get DNA from the VIC and some foreign DNA that we believe could possibly be the killer. Unfortunately, the results for the additional residue came back inconclusive, which is a bummer," Felicity explained.

"However, that doesn't mean we didn't get a few pings on some markers!" Dwayne added.

"What do you mean when you say a few pings?" one officer asked.

"Great question. Dwayne?" Felicity said as she stepped to the side.

"Ok, maybe this will help," Dwayne said as he fired up a PowerPoint. "As you can see, our markers indicate that our perp is a male, at least by birth genetics. Additionally, he is more likely than not Caucasian.

Given what we know, that at least cuts our demographic search down by quite a bit."

"Ok, seems we got all the brothers and the ladies off the hook, so what's the big news?" officer Jenkins belted out from behind me.

"Yes, of course," Dwayne said, adjusting his posture. "You're correct, Jenkins. We did eliminate the female populus almost entirely and persons of color. They're not entirely eliminated, but the likelihood is slim to none."

I shifted in my chair, regretting not grabbing some Gin to go with the coffee.

"The breakthrough news is this," Felicity explained. "Because of our ability to identify the victim, we determined that she lived close to the previous victim."

"And she may not have been a natural brunette," Dwayne added aggressively.

"How close would you say Victoria Wallace resided in relation to this new person?" I decided to interject to offer my hand in participating.

"Amazingly close. We've identified the new victim as Mary Richford. She lived in the same apartment complex, just at the opposite end set of buildings."

"So, a crime of opportunity?" I asked.

"Very much likely!" Dwayne said, taking back over. "That's all we know. The chief, captain and lieutenant will be developing a game plan to patrol the area and handling that portion of the brief. I just do forensics. Beyond that, that is all we have for you, and thanks for your time!"

Felicity walked over to me. "See me when you can."

I looked puzzled as she and Dwayne stepped out into the breezeway. *Christ. What could be so important that they need me to see them on a sidebar?*

I decided to excuse myself while Chief Whittiker rambled on about procedure, patrols, etc. The majority of that didn't apply to me, and if

I had anything to input, I would. I walked to the end of the breezeway to meet Forensics.

"Good, you're here. You look pretty good today. Special occasion?" Dwayne asked.

"Saw my kids this morning."

"Oh, shit! Did we pull you in from that? Because after this bit of info, we can just cover for you if you need a bit of time," Dwayne blurted with worry on his face.

I waved him off. "No worries. That was the longest I think I'd been present in a long time. What's the big news?"

"Ok, so it's just something we didn't want to boil out into the chatterbox of the bullpen, but we're engaged!" Felicity held up her ring finger.

"You and Dwayne?" I asked, confused.

"No, dummy. To Ricky! I'm gay, remember? Although now my future 'if this doesn't work out, we'll marry each other' plan is shot." Dwayne sassed.

"Oh, Jeeze. Am I out of the loop that bad? I'm so sorry," I grumbled. "Congratulation's you guys. I mean it."

"Wow. Don't sound so sincere, big guy. I just wanted to tell you since you're my favorite detective!"

It's true. We've been pretty tight-knit ever since we worked the Crazed Couple Killer case together. Felicity was like an older daughter to me. I should have expressed more emotion, but I was too dog shit tired to feel anything.

"I'm really happy for you, truly. I'm just dead on my feet right now. Mind if we celebrate tomorrow? I'm going to head home and try to catch up on some sleep and hope nothing new brings itself to light," I said, blinking my eyes to show my exhaustion. "Call me if something new happens, ok?"

Before we could part ways, Chief Whittaker stormed out of the conference room.

"Goddamnit! Another one! That's barely a day apart! This son of a bitch has a lot of time on his hands." Chief moved to the center of the building, cupping his hands to his mouth to project. "EVERYONE TO THE WAR ROOM, IMMEDIATELY! I DON'T GIVE A SHIT WHAT YOU'RE DOING!"

He glanced over at me before moving back into the war room. He thrust both doors open and stormed inside. I knew the look meant I wasn't going to bed for a while.

I watched everyone pour into the room. We knew time was of the essence, but we needed a quick briefing.

"Ok, new VIC. We think it's our guy. A few officers on patrol picked up some Korean man who was raving like a lunatic! Once they calmed him down, Officer Kim could translate enough to figure they found a new body."

"Jesus, a new one?" an officer yelled out.

"Yes, a new one. I need a team assembled immediately. Forensics, you'll be dispatched now. Grab your gear and go. Have Edna give the directions to you upfront. Since you've had your ear to the ground on this case, Morgan, you're lead. This is your baby now, don't fuck it up. The last thing I need are the feds up my ass for a serial killer case."

I honestly was too tired to be offended. I gave a half-ass two-finger salute to my temple as I turned to follow Felicity and Dwayne out. Ever since getting busted down to detective from a lead position, I hadn't been called on in some time. I personally requested the demotion given my circumstances, although I was clearly not in the mindset to make major life decisions.

"Mind if I ride with you guys? I want to catch a quick nap before we get there. I won't be any good to you otherwise," I said.

"Sure thing. We'll take my van so you can spread out," Dwayne said as we headed toward the parking lot.

I climbed into the back of Dwayne's van and laid down across the bench seat. I barely remember falling asleep, but it happened damn near immediate. The very next thing I recalled was Felicity waking me up. The look on her face was like she'd seen a ghost. I wasn't sure if the nap helped or if Felicity's expression jarred me awake, but I felt more alert than ever.

"What? What is it?" I asked as I climbed out of the van and composed myself.

"We went in early to get a fix on the scene. It's fucked up, man," Felicity said as she sat down on her haunches and rested her head between her knees.

For as long as I've known her, she's seen some crazy things. She was strong, and I was impressed by that fortitude, frankly. If this broke her, it must have been gruesome. Hell, I felt a bit of hesitation as I approached the building. I looked around at where I was. Because of my slumber, I missed out on the approach, which meant double the work for me when I case the scene. It was a busy enough area. It was a shopping center that had all but been decommissioned a few months ago. Inside there were three to five stores in the dying mall. I followed the police tape toward the side entrance of the abandoned anchor store.

Inside, I found Dwayne. He was clearly shaken but not nearly as bad as Felicity.

"Everything good?" I asked casually.

"Forward, past the two columns and to the right," Dwayne said as he stepped outside for some air.

I followed his instructions. I could see ghosts of the women's department all around, with a few empty mannequins, shelving, and even some signage. *Bras on sale, 20% off, this Saturday only!* As I muttered and commented to myself, reminiscing over the days Zahra and I used to shop here when we were younger, I turned the corner to the right. I fell backward into a display to catch myself.

Blood was sprayed from one end of the department to the other. I believe this was the "plus-size" area, but I couldn't be sure. I made a note of that just in case that was significant. O'Hurley's hadn't been around in nearly a decade, and this building has been vacant for about as long. They couldn't keep up with Penny's and Macy's, or even the Walmart that had just been erected the year before the store's demise. I collected myself before I moved into detective mode.

I took the entire scene in. There was no pattern in the blood. Nothing ritualistic, Satanic, or the sort. Just sprays of it everywhere. Carnage spattered damn near one hundred and fifty cubic feet. The whole department was saturated with mayhem. I can see why Felicity had to leave. Between the low lighting and the level of gore, this could become too much for anyone. Without anything obvious to discern, I moved through the scene, careful not to step in puddles or piles.

After a few steps, I came upon a mannequin that was carefully placed in the aisleway. The others were in disarray, broken, or toppled over. This one was deliberately moved. I withdrew my flashlight and moved toward the figure, complementing the natural light that poured through the large windows above me. As I approached, I noticed the mannequin had a head, unlike the others. *The victim's head.* I gagged a bit before getting myself under control. This asshole spiked this poor girl's head onto a damn dummy body. What kind of pervert psycho does that? Unfortunately, my next question would be easier to answer. Where the hell was the rest of her?

I tiptoed around the aisleways and carnage to find a hacksaw. There was some chewed gristle and skin stuck to the blades. We found a murder weapon or a tool the killer used to break down the bodies.

"Morgan? You in here?" a voice called from the entrance.

"Yo!" I yelled, waving my flashlight over my head to signal.

"We're cutting on the power. We've got the building manager here to help with that. Hold tight one moment!" The voice yelled. It sounded like Dwayne, but it could have been any officer, truthfully.

I sat tight, as instructed. A loud pop and buzzing erupted as hundreds of fluorescent bulbs fired up. Several blew due to old age, raining glass down at the other end of the store. As I turned to focus my attention on the matter at hand, I could now see just how horrific this scene was. The mannequins that I passed by earlier contained a part of this girl. One, a leg, the other, an arm. The other figure had an arm that possessed a missing hand. There was no other leg or torso to speak of. I stepped through the viscera and made my way back to the main walkway to greet Dwayne and Felicity as they approached.

"It's worse in the lighting," I groaned.

"It's out of me. There's no more vomit to produce," Felicity said as she pushed past me to the scene. "I saw the one arm on this thing, and I freaked. Sorry."

"Completely understandable!" I said, trying to console her as best as possible at this moment. "I'm going to take a look around further. There's no torso or left leg around here."

Dwayne shot a thumbs up to me as I turned to wander the store. I hadn't even moved upstairs yet. Blood was all over this place, and the Plus Size area was adjacent to the escalator. That was off, so I took the unpowered stairs as they were. Slowly, I moved up to the second floor, worried my perp would be lurking around for me. I whipped myself around once I had enough height to see; empty. Nothing but trash, open shelves, and memories.

One area stood out. Several oil drums, the kind you typically see in industrial yards or on the docks, were sitting idle in what appeared to be the electronics department. I drew my sidearm and approached with caution. I kept on a swivel, careful to not slip in the trail of blood as I moved forward. Inside, the barrel contained a chemical of unknown origin and the missing parts. A half-dissolved ribcage protruded just under a mostly burned-away breast.

"Up here! Bring the chem gloves!" I screamed toward the stairwell.

Moments later, two officers and Dwayne rushed up the stairs. Dwayne threw the large, black rubber gloves over his hands and hurried over to me, careful not to slip in the blood.

"What? What do you—" Dwayne stopped mid-sentence.

"Can you retrieve this quickly and carefully?" I asked as I stepped back from the barrels.

Dwayne, without hesitation, threw his hands around the shoulder and molten rib cage of the torso, ripping it from the vat of death. He half set down-tossed it onto the ground in front of him, the skin still sizzling. He returned to look into the vat for anything further, but nothing was found, it seemed.

"Christ, that was a rush!" Dwayne exclaimed as he threw the chem gloves off his hands and onto the floor, still sputtering.

I looked at the torso. There was visible bruising, a clear sign of a struggle. We didn't need Felicity to analyze this to know that, but she would.

"Can we get an ID on that compound, Dwayne?" I asked.

"On it!" he said as he rushed down the stairs toward his van.

I looked on at the deteriorated corpse. Poor girl. No one deserved this.

"Found the hand!" one of the officers exclaimed from behind me.

I followed his voice to an empty shelf. On it contained one pristine, practically untouched hand. No chemical burns, no bruising or cutting, save for the amputation mark on the wrist. I inched in closer, moving the hand slightly to the side with my flashlight. The fingernails had been plucked. That was the final straw for me. I dry heaved somewhat as I backed away. I retreated to the guard rail that overlooked the escalator and waited for Dwayne to return.

As Dwayne climbed the stairs, I signaled for him to see me.

"Over there, on that shelf. A hand. The missing one. Just so you don't miss it," I said, trying to be helpful under gagging reflexes.

Dwayne nodded. He approached the vat and using a set of tools, retrieved a sample of the chemical compound before heading to the hand.

"Morgan!"

I rushed to Dwayne, not sure what I would walk into.

"Morgan, did you see this?" Dwayne pointed to the fingertips.

"Yeah. I saw the fingernails were ripped off."

"Well, there's that, but look! Her fingerprints were burned off. The fingernails and tips were defaced, but otherwise, this hand is untouched."

I made a similar observation but didn't notice the fingerprints. This is why they were the forensics, and I wasn't.

"Jesus, these weren't plucked post-mortem, either. What a sick bastard!" Dwayne wheezed out through his disgust.

"Think this girl lived near the other two?" I asked out of general curiosity.

"Well, once we get an ID on her, we'll know for sure. We may be able to get an ID match from her head downstairs with missing persons if we're lucky. Her being a redhead sure shakes things up, doesn't it?" Dwayne surmised.

"Yeah, a bit. If this girl lives in the same apartments or vicinity as the others, we have our perp's target area. Otherwise, we're shit out of luck."

"This is kind of like the one case I trained on, back when I was just starting out. Some guy was picking up women from a community center, and they'd be found mutilated days later."

"Think this is a copycat? Why didn't you say something before?" I grumbled.

"Well, I talked to Felicity on the way over. Before, it didn't seem relevant, but I also didn't know that was a real historic case we had been working on,"

I put my flashlight away. "Look, if you get anything, please let me know. I'm going to try to go back home, clear my head, and eventually wrap it around this case."

"You do that. Get some sleep, buddy. We'll see you tomorrow," Dwayne said as I started down the escalator stairs.

Chapter 10

Becca lay naked beneath the covers beside me, and her breathing slowed until it reached the steady rhythm of sleep. I stayed awake long after sex and the multiple and prolonged good night kisses with too much on my mind. I seized my opportunity to slip out of the bed when she rolled over, pulling on my t-shirt and boxer shorts.

I grabbed my phone and wallet in which I'd slipped the nameless rookie's number, then headed to the living room. I hoped Becca wouldn't overhear this late-night conversation between a work-obsessed journalist and an unknown informant to a story.

I dialed the number, then sat on the sofa and listened to the phone ring. I was about to hang up by the fifth or sixth ring when the ringing stopped, and a man's voice answered.

"Is this the reporter with the Daily Sentry in Severna Village, Pennsylvania?"

"It is," I answered. "May I ask who this is?"

"No names, please," he said. "I know you respect your source's right to anonymity. If you need a name, you can call me Mike."

"Okay, Mike. You're taking a big risk talking to me. May I ask a motive?"

"It's nothing personal," he said. "I don't want fame or anything like that. It's just Parkside's little police blotter didn't do the public any justice. Here, let me read it to you."

"That's okay," I said. "I saw it. It was a joke. They warned citizens should be wary."

Mike scoffed. "You don't know the half of it. They're keeping the public in the dark. This guy is a monster."

"How do you know it's a guy?" I asked.

"I have your email address, Mr. Marks. When this conversation is over, I'll send you a photo for your story. Then you can decide on this monster's gender."

Then without further prompting, he went into vivid detail about every photograph he's seen and every crime scene he's been to. While his experience as a rookie cop was limited, I would've put my money down that he'd seen more than most seasoned veterans would see in their twenty to thirty years of service. I've included the conversation details in the piece I wrote for the Daily Sentry.

The Mutilator Strikes! 3 women dead, barely recognizable!

Parkside, Michigan. A quaint industrial town with a population just shy of 200 thousand, has come under terror as a serial killer runs rampant. Reports indicate a confirmed three victims and rising. Each victim bore a strong similarity to the previous. Shelly DuLong, a graduate student and mother of two. Christina MacDade, recently engaged to Joseph Satiana. Finally, Elizabeth Dorchester. Each woman found dismembered, disfigured, and mutilated beyond near recognition.

The common thread between these women is unclear. Each was a blonde, ranging in ages 24 to 38 years. Authorities are baffled as to how to handle the case, sources say. Reports indicate that the women were tortured for hours, enduring prolongued periods of limb removal, before meeting their final demise at the hands of the killer via a vat of unknown substance. Sources support that the substance boils the victims down. This explains reports of fingerprint removal of the victims. The hands were carefully removed and preserved, hidden within the crime scene.

One could speculate why the hands are significant. According to Aristotle, hands are considered the tool of tools. They symbolize strength, power, and protection. Perhaps this was a symbolic, ritualistic killing devised by a lunatic to seek out a higher power? It may also be a possibility the killer has maternal issues. The classic "mommy" syndrome so apparent in many killers of our time. Perhaps scorned by a lover, or quite possibly unhinged by the fact they never found one of their own.

As reports trickle in from Parkside, more to follow. Be sure to follow our social media pages for the latest updates on the Parkside Mutilator, as we are unofficially calling him here at the station.

"Work obsessed?" I heard Becca inquire from behind me.

I looked up from where I'd sunk at least two inches into the couch. Becca stood in the dim light between the kitchen and our bedroom, where she had draped herself in a fleece blanket.

"Seriously, Jas," she said. "Please don't tell me you're working on that story."

"You're right," I said as I saved the word document and opened outlook. "Let me just send this off to Griffin, and I'll come back to bed."

"Whatever," she said and turned, retreating into the darkness. I selected Griffin from my contacts dropdown and sent the email off with the file attached.

Then I waited. Knowing Griffin, he'd be nursing a bourbon and smoking a cigar in the dimly lit basement of his townhouse while his wife snored away somewhere upstairs. And I'm not wrong.

Minutes ticked by, and my email pinged with a prompt reply from Griffin.

"Spectacular! Striking! Amazing!" the email read. "This'll print in the Sunday edition. If it gains the attention, and I think it will — you and Patti will be heading off into the throes of action."

{ 11 }

Chapter 11

I'd never been happier to jab my key into the apartment door in my whole life. I pushed it open, which struggled against a ton of papers and two dozen beer and liquor bottles. I closed the door behind me and flipped on the light, even though the sun hadn't set quite yet. The city was quieter this evening, unusual for Parkside. I flopped down on the sofa, springing at least five beer bottles toward the floor. Looking around the apartment, I decided a housekeeping session was in order. I headed toward the kitchen for a few trash bags.

I must have cleaned up a few hundred beer bottles and half as many liquor bottles. As far as the eye could see, there were papers from takeout menus, pizza boxes, and Chinese food containers. I really let everything go, didn't I? That disaster took me three hours to clean, and I was drained. After hurling the last bag of bottles into the recycling dumpster, I made my way home. I walked back in, almost as if I saw a new place for the first time. I don't think I remember the last time I saw the floor or had been able to use the countertop. Hell, my bed was completely free and clear of anything. I planned to wash the sheets tomorrow.

I dropped my clothes off my body haphazardly near the closet door and made my way to the shower. Turning the knob, the hot water seemed to help wash the horrid things I'd seen today, if only slightly. I considered the idea of having a shower beer, but I was too exhausted to move back to the kitchen, figuring it be better to just get clean and grab some shut-eye.

I slid into the bed with ease. I sprawled out, lying on my side, and quickly fell asleep. The dreams kept coming. Some about Zahra, others with my kids. Then they swiftly turned to nightmares. Gunshots ringing out. Seeing Cooms gasping for breath as I held onto him in his final moments. The EMTs took their sweet time, in my mind. I know they moved as quickly as possible. I kept seeing Cooms repeatedly, asking me not to leave him. The look on his son's face at the funeral. Nightmares replayed in my mind over and over before the buzzing of my phone woke me up.

It was daylight outside. I had slept clean into the late morning. Fumbling for my phone, I saw it was Chief Whittaker.

"Yeah, Chief?" I said, answering the phone and trying not to sound like I had just woken up.

"You catch the news? This shit is all over! A Gotdamned media frenzy!" Chief barked.

I rubbed my eyes and tried to wake up some. "What is all over?"

"The Mutilator case, or whatever this fucking kid from PA is calling it! That's what!"

I put the chief on speakerphone and opened my social media. Sure enough, at least two of my friends had shared an article regarding the details of our case. Intimate details. Things the public wouldn't know.

"I'll be at the station shortly, and we'll see what we can do to get ahead of this," I suggested.

"Ahead of it? This whole thing has steamrolled right through a dog-gone news station!" Chief belted.

"I see an article online about the case from our local news. Is that it?" I asked.

"Some kid named Jasper. Some upstart, up-and-coming moron thought he'd get the scoop and gave out information, including the victims' names! We hadn't even gotten to talk to the latest one's family! I've got them in the station up my ass about protocol and sloppiness. Get your ass down here!" Chief said as he hung up the phone.

Who the hell got this clown the information? I read through the article to see how detailed it was, and the chief was right. They had the names, the details — everything. Jesus H! What the hell were we going to do about this? I continued to thumb through the article. A photo marked "explicit content hidden, log in and click to unhide" slid by. I created a quick account. What should have been a brisk breeze had me making an asinine fake account on some internet news site. After confirming my account, I swiftly returned to the article, swiping to the image.

The body. It was the goddamned body! I threw my phone down in frustration at seeing one of our forensic photos used as some smut piece to grab some likes before retrieving it again. I had to know what asswagon wrote this. I went to the bottom of the article. Below the like, subscribe, and follow jargon, there it was: the source. Some guy named Jasper Marks. I leaped out of bed, ripped open my closet, and threw some clean clothes on before rushing to the station. I was boiling with several emotions including fear, anger, hatred, and something darker and more sinister.

I must have sped through a half dozen yellow lights. I didn't want to waste time getting to the station. I had the music turned off, a sure sign I was not in a good mood. Thankfully, I heard my phone buzzing in the cupholder next to me.

"Morgan," I said as I answered without looking.

"Steer clear of the station, detective. The goddamn buzzards are thick outside, trying to get anyone to say anything about the case. We've got our media team working to take care of it. Lay low for the day and keep where I can reach you when I need you. I can't believe this doggone shit."

Chief hung up after beginning a tirade of swears. I pulled into a Burger King parking lot and collected myself. I had been trying to get to work and driving aggressively that I needed to cool off. I needed to calm down. I started thumbing through my phone and dialing the one number I probably shouldn't have.

"Kurt? Are you ok?" Zahra asked from the other end of the line.

"I'm fine. Are you and the kids safe?" I asked, a bit of worry in my voice.

"We are. I guess you saw the news. Is that your case?"

I hesitated. There was no lying to Zahra, and it seemed like she already knew the deal. I gave it to her straight.

"It is. How much did you see of it?"

"Enough to know that maybe you should stop by the house for a few when you can."

"How about now?" I asked.

I knew going to see the kids and being in a warm environment might be what I needed to do. I felt bad that I ran out early the other day. I owed them at least three showings of Frozen.

"If that works for you. We were about to have lunch. Want me to set you a place?" Zahra asked.

Her voice sounded positive. Setting a place for me at the table hasn't been done in so long; I think it felt like the most normal thing to happen in the past few days.

"That's fine. I'll be there in twenty. See you soon."

"Ok, see you soon. I—I'll see you when you get here," Zahra said, hanging up the phone quickly.

I've been guilty of nearly saying I loved her more than a dozen times. This may have been her first slip-up. I was slightly more eager to get to the house now more than ever. I went to the nearby grocery store and picked up a small pie and a bouquet of flowers before making my way to the house. I wanted to arrive with a peace offering. I wanted to make this right.

I pulled up to the house, greeted by my two children and Zahra waiting on the front step.

"Daddy!" Alisa said as she rushed toward me.

I scooped my daughter up in a giant swoop and spun her around. Davey seemed unphased one way or the other at my presence.

"We're having breakfast for lunch!" Alisa shouted excitedly in my ear.

I set Alisa down as she quickly latched to my leg. I pulled open the back passenger car door as best as I could.

"Go with your mother. I'll be inside in a moment, sweetie."

"You better, mister!" Alisa said as she put her hands on her hips. She had her mother's sass, that was for sure.

I reached into the back seat and retrieved the pie and flowers before starting for the house. Inside smelled like waffles and bacon, my favorite. I produced the pastry first, handing it to Davey, who un- enthusiastically set it on the counter beside him before sitting at the table. Finally, I presented the flowers.

"Really? Flowers? Isn't that a bit cheeseball?" Zahra asked as she took them.

"They're for the table," I said, forming a pretty quick excuse.

Zahra set the flowers on the countertop next to the pie and took a seat at the table. I grabbed the seat at the head of the antique white- wash table. I loved the color scheme of the kitchen. Antique whitewash was the color of choice. It was so bright and hopeful, unlike the dark and drab colors in the apartment. I quickly grabbed the fork and dug in. The waffles were still warm and soft. I can tell that they may have just started making food and stopped when I called.

"You smell good, Daddy! Like the waffles," Alisa said with a smile and a giggle.

I smirked a bit. "That's because daddy just got out of the shower and didn't have to go to work today, honey."

Zahra looked over at me. "You haven't...you know?"

I knew what she meant. It'd been a few days since I had a drink, which was pretty good for me. Above all, I think that was the reason she left me. She could deal with everything else but would not stand by as I killed myself little by little with the bottle.

"Actually, no. It's been a few days, and I feel pretty good!" I said proudly.

"You look good," Zahra said.

"Whatever," Davey grumbled as he shoved half a waffle into his mouth.

"Watch your tone, young man! Do not disrespect your father in this house. He works too damn hard for you to give this attitude!" Zahra snapped.

"Sure. He'll just leave again. Why don't you just let him pass out on the couch? He loves to do that. I bet my friend Timmy's dad has some booze for him."

"David Aymen Morgan! You will apologize to your father this instant!" Zahra commanded.

"Whatever. I'm not hungry anyway," Davey said as he stormed off for his bedroom.

"I'm so sorry, Kurt. He's been like this since—"

"I get it," I interrupted. "I'll go talk to the boy if it would help."

"Give him time to cool off. Meanwhile, don't let your food cool!" Zahra instructed, poking her fork in my direction.

I had to say, it had been a while since I enjoyed this kind of life. I may not even remember getting together this often, as it were. Work often got in the way. Part of me wondered if I could keep on this path and fix things with everyone. After sorting this case out, I'd put in my packet to retire and leave all of that mess behind. Move the family far from this place and get a quiet, remote house. Possibly take up fishing. Maybe teach Davey how to fish. Something my old man passed down to me.

I finished my food and watched as Alisa darted off to the den to fire up her favorite movie. I heard the infamous Disney logo music chime and knew this was the first of many playthroughs Zahra would endure if she hadn't been through a handful already.

"Step outside to talk?" I asked.

"Sure. We can sit out back on the porch swing if you'd like. It's a beautiful day today."

She was right. The weather was lovely. It was a moderately perfect day aside from an absolute boiling over pot of shit back at work and this killer on the loose. Things were starting to come up for me, it seemed. I followed Zahra outside to talk. We walked to the porch swing, which comfortably sat three people. I sat on one end, and Zahra curled up on the other.

"I read the articles. How is the case going?" Zahra inquired, cutting right to the chase.

"They're going. We need a break in the case, to be honest. This media frenzy is only going to make it worse."

"Oh? I'm sure that's not helping anyone get things done around there. How is Felicity?"

"She's great. Actually, she's engaged."

Zahra sat up excitedly. "She is! That is wonderful!" She sat back down and changed her expression. "How long have you known? Did you keep this from me?"

I smiled. "I only knew since yesterday, don't worry. I'll make sure Fel sends you an RSVP when the time comes."

"Thank you for that."

"For what?"

"Thinking of me. You always did manage a way through all of your time at work to do something like that. The little surprises. The little notes," Zahra said, lighting up a bit when she did.

I loved seeing her happy. Her smile and laugh were her best quality. Her olive skin glistened in the sunlight as we swung gently in the breeze. Her bright hazel eyes twinkled as she swayed back and forth, catching the light perfectly each time.

"And I missed your laugh. Think we could ever be on good terms again?" I asked.

Zahra sat up. "We were never on bad terms, Kurt. You just chose work and the bottle over us. You made that decision."

"I wish I could unmake that decision. I really screwed up."

Zahra put her feet down to stop the swing and stood up. "Well, you can start by talking to Davey."

I nodded and stood up. My phone buzzed as I grabbed the back doorknob. I glanced at the ID, and it showed Dwayne. I could feel Zahra giving me a look. I pressed ignore and proceeded on my path to talk to Davey. As I reached the stairs, my phone vibrated a second time. This time, it was Felicity. I ignored it and made my way up the stairs. As I reached the landing, my phone buzzed again; it was the chief. I had to decide: do I answer the phone, or do I patch things up with my son? Ignoring one or the other had extraneous repercussions. I decided to hit the button on the chief and rapped against my son's bedroom door.

"Go away!" Davey yelled from the other side.

"I'll have you know I ignored my boss on the phone to have this chat. I have to go back to work but wanted to talk to you."

"Fine. Come in. Whatever."

I entered the room slowly as if expecting booby traps or something. Davey was across the room on his laptop, scrolling up and down Twitter. I saw what he was looking at. It was the case. It was the crime photo.

"Listen, Davey. You don't need to—"

"Is this what's been going on? This is horrible, Dad!" Davey exclaimed. "You need to catch this asshole!"

"You're right. And don't use that language in this household. Even though the guy is an asshole," I said. I sat on the edge of his bed. "I need to go into work to find this *asshole*, Davey. After, we can do whatever you want to do. You name it, buddy."

Davey swiveled around in his chair. He had a high-end gaming chair we got him a few years ago. He'd been big into playing his video games and felt that a fancy chair would make him a better player. After much discussion, we splurged. When I was little, we had a floor. There was a couch close enough to the wired controllers if we were lucky.

"Is this why you were always gone? Why you're always messed up? That picture is pretty messed up, dude."

"You're right, buddy. It is. I was there. It's much worse in person. That's the whole reason I came up here to talk to you. It wasn't ever about ignoring you. I love you, your sister, and your mother very much. I just can't let guys like this get away. You understand that?"

"Is what this article says true?" Davey asked.

"Some of it. I'm going to work to figure out what we need to do about this article. Can we talk after?"

"I guess. You better come by to talk."

"Davey, you have my promise. I'm kind of glad you saw this. Don't tell your mother, though."

I stood up to leave, immediately entangled in two arms that thrust around me for a hug. I hadn't hugged Davey since he was a little guy. I threw one arm around his back and patted it, embracing him for a moment before he let go. I decided that was the opportune time to head back to the station. As I left the house, I called Felicity back.

"Fuck! What the hell took you so long? Chief is on a rampage! He thinks *we* leaked the photo to the reporter!" Felicity snapped immediately.

"Wait, what? What's going on?"

"The photo. Chief says we were the only ones that could have sent that off, and he's chewing Dwayne's ass right now as we speak. I can't lose my job! How will I pay for this wedding?"

I switched ears for my phone and drove a bit faster. "Calm down; nobody is getting fired. If we didn't share the photos, are you saying we have a mole that leaked the info?"

"I didn't even think about that. I immediately assumed someone hacked my camera somehow."

"That's not how these things work, Felicity. I'm on my way, I'll be there in a bit, and we can get things sorted out."

"Ok, hurry up. I don't know how much more of this we can take before Chief does something drastic," Felicity said as she hung up.

I eased my foot a bit more on the gas, worried for my two best forensics guys. I know for sure they didn't send out the photo. The real question was: who did?

{ **12** }

Chapter 12

I reached into my inside blazer pocket, and my hand closed on an envelope. I pulled it out to find my name scrawled on the front. I didn't recognize the handwriting.

"Sir?"

I looked around. A line at the coffee shop had formed behind me, and the barista offered me a charitable smile. "Sir, I recommend the house blend."

I waved the barista off, stepped out of line, slid a finger through the envelope flap, and tore it open. I pulled out the note inside and took a seat at one of the empty tables.

> *Listen, Jas. Is it okay if I call you that?*
>
> *Doesn't matter. I read your little story, and I appreciate that you refrained from calling me a monster. With time, maybe you'll change your tune. Most do. Mommy issues, eh, Jas? That's a good guess. What'd you do? Look it up in your Psych 101 textbook? Even a middle schooler could've guessed that one. Ha! Mommy issues! I don't even think about the bitch. Not since finding her lifeless husk after she choked to death on the lung cancer-induced cigarettes she used to burn me with. A word of advice, give up the shit if you currently smoke. But I digress.*

> *Your information is second-hand and speculative, at best. If you want to know the truth, I'm surprised that asshole boss of yours printed it. Is your paper that hard up? Speaking of truth, why don't you step up your game a bit? You know, get a closer look at where the action really happens. I betcha you'll get off on that and write the story of a lifetime. Speaking of getting off. Why don't you bring that pretty little lady friend of yours along? And I'm not talking about the dyke you're writing this story with. You and Becca need a little time alone, don't you? Just the two of you? Aw, hell! Why not make a threesome? Bring that Patti chick along with you. But, in all seriousness, Jas. You need to get serious about your reporting, and I'm just the one to get you there. But you'll have to do something for me if this exchange will work properly. Interested? I'll see you around Parkside, Michigan. Your boss'll love you for it.*
> *Signed*
> *"The Mutilator"*
> *P.S. The nickname sucks.*

By the time I got to the end of the letter, my heart was racing. Even if the letter were a hoax, this guy had intimate knowledge about my personal life and seemed to know precisely what G. Greyson Griffin would be interested in reading and seeing.

My phone pinged.

Jasper, a text from Patti read, *where the hell are you? Meetings started, and Griffin looks pissed.*

I slipped my phone and the letter into my pocket, then hauled ass to The Sentry, dodging a few pedestrians on the walkway and inadvertently elbowing others.

Out of breath, I paused outside the newsroom just long enough to compose myself. When I opened the door, I caught the tail-end of Griffin's speech.

"—picking up. I can feel it, especially with Jasper's and Patti's recent story. Traffic on our website is by four hundred percent, but we're going to have to keep it that way." Griffin glared at me until several sets of eyes, Patti's included, turned in my direction. "Look who showed up. Marks, Patti, into my office. Everyone else, go find something newsworthy."

Griffin marched off toward his office, leaving Patti and me to gawk at each other. "What's gotten into him?"

Patti shrugged. "He's had a bug up his ass all morning."

We joined Griffin in his office, where his face had already taken a darker shade of pink as he paced back and forth, not bothering to look at either of us. "Lawyers up my ass. This is a media shit-show. Parkside police and this unknown agency claim a leak and threaten to sue if we don't reveal our source.'

"But they can't —"

"Of course, they can't," Griffin cut Patti off as he turned to face us. "Tell me you've got a plan to keep this thing going."

I hesitated, if only for a moment, then pulled the mysterious envelope out from my pocket and handed it to Griffin. "I found this on me this morning."

"What's that supposed to mean?" Griffin asked as he unfolded the letter. I didn't bother to explain how any number of people I bumped into, including the guy who dropped his briefcase, could have slipped the note inside my pocket. Besides, Griffin had already immersed himself in the letter, chuckling in spurts as his eyes scanned the page.

Patti leaned over to me and whispered. "Is this what held you up?"

I nodded, and Griffin took a seat and grinned. "You know what this means? We've got the eyewitness account of the serial killer. That's what it means. Do you two think you can handle this?"

"I don't even know what this is," Patti said. "Can I see the letter?"

We gave her a moment to read, then she responded. "What the hell? He's taunting us now? He doesn't even know us?"

"So, are you in?" I asked.

"You know I am," Patti said, then turned to Griffin. "Greyson, what do you think?"

"I think the Bobbsey twins couldn't hold a candle to you two," Griffin said. "Get yourselves packed and ready to go. I'll have my secretary book you two a flight early tomorrow morning."

"If you don't mind, sir," I said. "I'll need to head out later in the week."

Patti's eyes narrowed while Griffin waved my request off with, "Fine. Whatever. Just get boots on the ground as soon as you can."

Patti and I said our thanks and turned to leave.

"Just remember," Griffin said. "I want pictures."

Chapter 13

I hadn't gotten two steps into the bullpen before I heard the chief clear his throat to speak.

"Morgan! Right now! My office!"

I don't think I had moved as quickly as I did since my days in the academy. Hell, I don't think I could hustle like this while I *was* in the academy! I brushed past officers who did nothing but stare in my direction as if I was making my way down The Green Mile. I was about to be fried for a crime I didn't commit. At least, that's how I saw it. As I rounded the corner, I could see Felicity and Dwayne sitting in front of the chief's desk, receiving the ass chewing of a lifetime. I thrust open the door. I thought about saying something witty, like, "you wanted to see me, sir?" I felt the point was moot and likely won't be well received.

"Sit the fuck down with the other two, Morgan!" Whittaker boomed.

I felt like I was in grade school, and this was the principal's office. I had enough information from Felicity to avoid being blindsided, but I was not prepared for this firing squad of questioning. I quickly sat on the rolling stool next to the fish tank Chief always maintained in his office.

"Jesus H! What the hell am I supposed to do?" Chief demanded, rubbing the bridge of his nose in frustration before standing up dramatically. "Who the hell is Jasper Marks?"

I perked up slightly. Felicity and Dwayne looked dumbfounded, so I chimed in.

"I heard he had all kinds of information and wrote a fluff piece about this case. My son pulled up an article before I came over here," I stammered out before composing myself.

Chief paced around the room a bit. "What's his connection to you? Is he a buddy? Giving you a huge payday? A cut at the novel? Royalties or a walk-on role for the movie? Huh? What is it?"

I stood up. "No idea, sir. I wish I knew this joker."

"What do you mean you don't know him? You three don't know him, but you were the only one with access control to his photos? Bullshit. Give me something else to chap my ass."

"He's serious. We don't know the guy! I told Detective Morgan earlier that we might have someone internal who leaked the file and reports," Felicity jutted into the conversation.

Chief quickly whipped around and slapped both hands on his desk in frustration. "Well, then who the flying monkey shit is it?"

I paused for a moment. I cycled through every possible avenue that one of our officers or associates would take to leak information to some half-cocked journalist from across the country. I couldn't drum up a single viable candidate. Everyone had a reason, whether they were sick of the day-to-day or hard-pressed for a raise that wasn't coming. Anyone under this roof had a valid motive.

"Listen. I'll be as plain as I can right now, Morgan," Chief said as he collected himself and sat at his desk. "If—and I mean *if* you see this clown, Jasper Marks, at a single crime scene: bring him in at all costs. I won't just throw the book at him; I'll beat him to death with it and scrape up the paste left behind with the book's cover."

The way the chief said the last bit was unsettling. Honestly, that may be an understatement, only rivaled by the gore witnessed with this Chemical Burn killer. It wasn't so much what he said but *how* he said it. Calm, as if he came to terms with what he'd genuinely do. I knew it was just a ruse and something to say in the heat of the moment, but what if? I zoned out a bit at the thought of Chief being the killer.

"Morgan?" Felicity said, snapping me back to reality.

"Oh, yeah. What?" I said as I collected myself and focused.

"We're going to head out. We need to figure out where and how to find this Jasper guy and get ahead of this. He could be the killer or an inside source. Either way, the fact that we just got an ass chewing for his shenanigans really jerks my chicken," Dwayne joked while being extremely serious.

Chapter 14

Becca and I arrived in Parkside, Michigan a few days later. It took me that long to convince her that Parkside would be the small-town dream destination she didn't know she wanted to visit. It took the jewelry store that long to convince her it would run smoothly without her. Within that time, my co-journalist, Patti, had already set up shop in one of the bed and breakfasts within a brightly painted Victorian home overlooking the lake. She arranged for similar accommodations for Becca and me a few blocks away. All of this on The Daily Sentry's dime, of course. Somehow Patti and I planned to coordinate our movements to keep Becca in the dark about the real reason for the trip.

I shot Patti a quick text to let her know we'd settled into our place on the third floor. Though its exterior showed its turn-of-the-century age, the room was equipped with all the modern amenities from free wi-fi, which I planned to use often, and free television on a 65-inch which I planned to never turn on.

The toilet flushed in the bathroom located in our room suite. Moments later, the door opened just as I finished my exchange with Patti. I turned, and Becca swayed toward me, wrapping me in her embrace. Between kisses, Becca and I made plans.

"First," she said, "you've really outdone yourself. I don't know how, but I suspect you —"

I kissed her. "Don't overthink it. This place, this town, it's beautiful."

"I know," she said, kissing me. "But don't think I'm not onto you."

My heart skipped a beat as I realized for the first time this would also be an excellent setting for an engagement. I gave her a wink. "I wouldn't expect anything less. Shall we tour the town?"

Like many lakefront towns, Parkside's industrial uses dried up sometime in the 80s. An ancient mall located five miles from the city's center went the way of the city's industry. I was dying to check out the dead mall where The Mutilator's latest victim had been scattered over the length of a department store. But I knew that slight detour was out of the question. For now, I had to be content with enjoying Parkside's skyline, which consisted of a mixture of skeletal remains of once-bustling factories and recently revitalized warehouses converted into mixed-use corporate centers and pricey condos. This view took up about twenty-five percent of the city's prime real estate, whereas the main attraction — the city center — was only a few blocks away.

Becca and I took a slow stroll through the neighborhood in which one Victorian home seemed to blur with another until we came to rows of colonials, then row homes and shops. Parkside's downtown consisted of boutique shops, antique stores, and an array of restaurants that would satisfy anyone's culinary needs. Ahead, I spotted Patti making her rounds, and I yanked Becca into the first store we came to. The door chimed as we walked in, and I went to a dead stop when I took in the glass cabinetry and the sparkle of jewelry.

An older gentleman in a three-piece suite greeted us. Becca answered with a nudge in my rib.

"We're just browsing," I told the man.

He gave me a knowing nod. "Perhaps the lady would like to take a look at the necklaces or rings?"

"That'll be nice, wouldn't it, Jasper?"

Becca tried on half a dozen rings, then we thanked the gentleman for his help.

"It's been my pleasure," he said, slipping me his business card. "Hope to see you soon."

Becca wrapped an arm around me. "What're you planning next, stud?"

"Just browsing is all," I replied, rather coy. We walked through the door and I had an epiphany. "I gotta take a leak. Mind waiting a sec?"

"Hurry up. You're lucky the weather is nice," Becca replied, pulling out her phone to kill a few moments.

I dashed inside and hailed the clerk who waited on us.

"Back already, I see?" the sales clerk asked.

"The last ring she tried. It fit perfectly. Can I get that wrapped and ready to go?" I said, producing my credit card quickly and discretely. "May I use your restroom, if you don't mind?"

The clerk seemed happy and defeated in the same expression. "Through the curtain, on your left."

Once I emerged back into the store, the clerk had my ring neatly packaged in a bag with my card in hand. I grabbed the ring box from the bag and my credit card and smiled. I jammed the box into my pants pocket, and put my card back into my wallet, returning to Becca.

"Everything ok?" Becca joked.

"Business as usual, if that's what you're asking. I'm good to go now," I said, nodding toward the remaining shops.

The street sloped down toward the lake, with many more shops and restaurants to explore. But there was one place I needed to check out. "We'll be here for the next several days. I'm thinking we can window shop as we head down to grab lunch from this bistro I heard about."

Several blocks later, accompanied by commentary from Becca about how she wanted to stop at this shop or the next on our way back, we came to the last of the rowhomes. After this, the city block hooked a right, around which warehouse apartments mingled with a working industrial complex overlooking the lake.

"Patisserie's Bakery and Bistro," Becca mused. "Is this it?"

I turned. "Yeah... This is it."

Becca raised an eyebrow, then waited for me to open and hold the door for her. When I followed her inside, I locked eyes with Patti's wide-eyed expression as she turned in an attempt to make herself scarce. It didn't work.

"Patti!" Becca cheered. In a few short strides, she closed the distance between herself and the still stunned Patti. Then Becca wrapped her arms around her, kissing her on both cheeks.

"Becca," Patti said, taking a step back. "It's... uh... surprise to see both of you here." She shot me a narrow-eyed side look.

"It is," I said.

Becca sighed. "Save it. Both of you. I know about your Mutilator, and I have this feeling this particular out-of-the-way location has something to do with the killings."

A few heads turned. "You're right, Becca."

"Of course, I'm right," Becca said. "But since we're here, I plan to enjoy myself with or without you. How's that?" She looked from me to Patti.

When neither of us answered, Becca continued. "There's plenty of town for me to explore, Jasper. But I'm telling you one thing, the moment this work trip for you bleeds into my personal life, I'm out."

"Fair enough. We'll be able to cover more ground with two of us." I looked to Patti.

"Becca, I'll make sure Jasper has plenty of time with you." Patti grinned. "I also hear there's this luxurious day spa you would absolutely love."

Becca sat and picked up a menu. She then gave me a sly smile. "Well, are we eating or not?"

I took a seat. "Of course... order anything you like."

Patti remained standing. "I just ate, thanks. Jasper, I'll catch up with you later."

After Patti left, Becca and I soon ordered our food. Not surprisingly, Becca ordered the most expensive item, Steak Frites, leaving me to cut back on the bill by ordering hors d'oeuvres in the form of some forgettable eggplant dish.

When our meals came, Becca looked with pity upon me. "Both of our meals look and smell amazing. Let's share."

I grinned with relief, and both our dishes burst with flavor. Throughout the meal, we commented on the various shops we'd passed. With the afternoon still young and the evening far from us, we decided to head back to our bed and breakfast a different route.

The leisurely stroll back was anything but as it seemed, every other visitor appeared to have a similar idea. Mentally, I kicked myself as I realized fears would be heightened, and residents would want to get any kind of business accomplished while in groups and during the daylight. Becca and I managed to avoid running into most groups, while some seemed intentional about running into us with a bump here and a brush there.

We passed by an alluring old fountain, nestled gently in between several decorative topiaries. A wrought iron bench sat in front. I motioned Becca toward the bench.

"What's this about?" she asked.

Before Becca could turn to face me, I'd dropped to a knee. "Becca, will you marry me?"

I gazed up at Becca, who returned a shocked look. "Jesus, Jasper!" She took a few looks around at a half dozen gawkers. "Here? Right now?"

"No better time than the present, right?" I said confidently.

"I mean, this place, I—"

"It's beautiful, right?" I interjected. "Well?"

I started to slide the ring toward her ring finger as I held her hand. Becca hesitated momentarily, taking another look at her adoring audience.

"I—sure."

I slid the ring onto Becca's finger and stood up. Smiling, I took her hand in mine and we continued down the road back to our B&B.

By the time we got back to the bed and breakfast, I intended to call it a night as I unlocked the door, but Becca had other plans. As soon as the door shut, she cozied up to me and cooed. "Did you know the shower is built for two?"

I thought about what to say. She must have been in shock from the proposal earlier, but warmed up to me during the walk. Stage fright can do that. I played into her mood as best as I knew how.

"I may have noticed that," I snuggled closer to her.

She slipped away from me and pulled her top over her head with deliberation. She stopped at the bathroom door. "Well?"

"Warm it up for me," I said.

"Uh-huh," she cooed, then disappeared into the bathroom. A moment later, I could discern the sound of water running.

I turned to lock the door. As I did, my foot scuffed and slipped on the floor. I looked down and found myself standing on an envelope. I bent down and opened it.

Hey, tiger. Glad you made it. Check your pockets.

I did so and found a flip phone in the front pocket of my blazer. I closed my eyes in an attempt to visualize everyone we brushed against on our way back to the bed and breakfast. Somehow, the killer or someone managed to slip this on me. I had to be more diligent in the future.

"Jasper," Becca called over the flow of the shower. "You coming in, or what?"

"Just locking up," I called back.

I flipped open the phone to find a single text *I'll be in touch.*

I hit dial, but it immediately connected to the messaging system. *The number you are trying to reach is not in service. Please try again later.*

I secured the phone and the envelope in the bottom drawer of the entry table and then headed to the bathroom. The shower cut off just as I entered the bathroom. Becca reached her hand out from behind the curtain.

"It's about time, Jas," she said, "but I'm already finished. Hand me a towel, will ya?"

I did. "Sorry about that, there was —"

"No!" Becca said, sliding the curtain open. She already had the towel wrapped around her. She gave me a once-over of my nakedness. "It's a shame. It could have been fun. But that's what happens when you let work bleed over into your personal life."

She stepped out of the shower. "Get cleaned up. We're meeting Patti at Apex Fusion."

"That sounds like a dance club," I groaned.

She slapped me on my bare ass. "That's because it is. Get moving, buster. We're making the most of our time together."

As I showered, I wondered when Becca and Patti made plans to meet up at some random club.

That evening, Becca and Patti shouted at me over the club music. I didn't hear what either said, but I saw what they did. Becca grabbed Patti by the hand and led her out to the dance floor. They both were sexy as hell in their short skirts and halter tops. Becca's dark hair hung loosely at her shoulders, a stark contrast to Patti's platinum blonde pixie cut. As they danced together, I moseyed to the bar where I ordered myself a double bourbon, downed it at once, and ordered another. I wanted no part of Becca trying to make me jealous while she danced with my coworker, who, I hoped, was just keeping her distracted.

I nursed the second bourbon and pulled out my smartphone and earbuds. I placed one of the earbuds into my ear and opened the police scanner app. Familiar and worn-out 10-codes hit the earbuds as I sipped my drink, letting it slosh between my teeth. I choked on the next sip when a 10-54 came through — *Possible Dead Body.* Then a call for all units to a location. I punched the place into the maps and realized I was practically sitting on top of the crime scene.

Dropping a twenty on the bar top, I slipped out of the stool and headed downstairs. Sirens blared in the distance as I hit the warm-night air. I rechecked the map, then spotted flashlights coming to a stop a block away. I had to make it quick. Creep into the crime scene, snap a few photos, then get out and back to the club.

Three cruisers were parked, and one officer just began roping off the scene. I ducked behind a cruiser and spotted the scene some twenty yards away. Blood splattered adjacent walls of the alleyway The nexus of the splatter: a limbless and headless torso. A childhood experiment came to mind in which we dropped a Barbie from a third-story window, and I knew the Barbie fared much better than this poor woman.

I nudged myself forward and lurched behind a neighboring fence. From there, I took a few photos with my phone.

I zoomed in and I spotted a mysterious liquid dripping on the concrete. As it hit the ground, it sizzled. I needed to get a closer look. I dodged around the crime scene until I came to a gate. From there, I observed a small gathering of Parkside's finest. This angle also gave me a better look at the sizzling goo.

I snapped a photo, and the flash seemed to illuminate the entire crime scene unnecessarily. "Shit! Come on," I said a little too loudly.

Chapter 15

I hadn't had enough time to jab my key into the deadbolt before my phone started vibrating in my jacket pocket. I threw the door open, tossing the keys on the small table by the entryway. For the first time in a long time, it didn't ricochet off a half dozen beer bottles. I heard a simple ka-chank of the keys and a gentle slide as they landed. I used my free hand to reach for my phone as I closed the door behind me with my right foot.

"Morgan," I answered.

"Is that how you answer the phone for me?"

"Jesus, Zahra! I'm so sorry. My hands were full, and I have a lot—"

"I know," Zahra interrupted. "You seemed a bit out of it the other day."

I removed my wallet and badge and dropped them on the kitchen countertop, which doubled as a breakfast nook. It was still sticky from stale beers and spills, but this may have been the first time I'd seen the surface in ages. I moved toward the sofa in the living room and flopped down. I didn't even bother removing my jacket.

"Someone leaked info from the station," I said bluntly, knowing she could handle anything I threw at her.

"Wait, like— a mole?" Zahra asked.

"Just like in the spy movies," I said, rubbing my forehead in frustration. "We don't know who it is. I spent the better part of the afternoon getting my ass chewed."

Silence greeted me on the other line for a moment before she spoke. "Did he think it was you?"

I let out a nervous little laugh. "I honestly don't know what to believe at this point. Whittaker was tearing through all of us like no tomorrow. I just think I was in the crosshairs due to my proximity to the case."

"Jeeze. I thought he would take it easy on you after everything with, you know."

"Cooms?" I finished.

"Yeah. I don't think you quite got past that, and your chief saw that. Didn't he?"

"I honestly don't know. Taking leave and getting away from the case and his death only made me feel more useless."

I felt my phone give a slight vibration. I pulled it away from my face to see a call coming in from Felicity.

"Hey, I have to go. Work is on the other line."

"I get it. Just be safe. Can we meet up for lunch or dinner tomorrow? Work free? Just you and I?" Zahra asked.

I was floored. Did she want to go on a date? That's how I saw it, at least. "Sure, you bet! Let me get to this."

I pressed the call button to transfer to Felicity.

"Morgan! Jesus Christ, he's done it again! You need to get down here. I think it's our guy again," she belted out.

"Ok, give me a few and text me the address. I'll be there," I said, standing up and buttoning my jacket.

I guess part of me assumed there was no rest for the weary. I made for the door and found myself bound for another crime scene. My mind went on autopilot as I navigated the familiar city streets, passing by local shops and hurrying pedestrians. I had lost track of time. If someone pulled up next to me and asked if I knew what day it was, I, honest to God, couldn't tell them. Was it Tuesday? It felt like a Tuesday. Glancing at my phone briefly while at a red light, I confirmed that it was in fact Friday. I shook myself out of the funk that overwhelmed me and drove on, only taking a break to hit the gas station for two Redbull drinks. This may be the first time I've tasted the beverage without some kind of alcohol drowning it out. Honestly? It tasted like shit. How do the kids just drink these things down?

I pulled into a gated community. The GPS said I was right. Some new condo development, likely bulldozed over some cheap houses to make way for overpriced gentrification. Capitalism at its finest. I rolled my window down to greet the guard with my badge. He got up from his booth, meeting me at the car window to view my credentials.

"Real nasty up there, Officer," the guard said, shaking his head.

"It's Detective."

"Oh. Really sorry about that one, Detective,"

"No worries," I said, putting the badge back in place and preparing to drive off. "Say, you wouldn't happen to know any details? Access control issues? Strange visitors?"

The guard took off his patrol cap for a moment. "Listen, I told the lady officer that I'd swing through the station after my shift and give a full statement."

I nodded in agreement.

"I'm working on getting the higher-ups to pass off the last two days' tapes to you guys. Best I can do," the guard said, shrugging his shoulders.

I paused for a moment. I wanted to drown him in a deluge of questioning but felt he'd had enough. The guard was just trying to do his job, and likely, he'll make good on his word to swing by the station. "I appreciate it."

I started to drive forward as the gate swung open.

"Hey, Detective? Up two streets, then make a right. Should be able to see everything at that point once you round the bend."

I gave him a two-finger to the forehead salute and nodded before driving off. His demeanor seemed pleasant, yet I found it off-putting given the circumstances. As I drove through the neighborhood, I was taking it all in. These were townhome-style condos. Visible line of sight throughout the entire community. There wasn't something you couldn't do without at least three neighbors seeing you in your yard or front window. If I was a betting man, this overpriced heap was likely going for half a million bucks per house to start.

I rounded the corner as instructed. I passed by a jogger with their dog. Another lady struggled with trying to cram her kid into a car seat. Everything seemed disturbingly business as usual. Then I rounded the bend. A calamity of squad cars, forensics vehicles, police tape, and about two dozen officers polluted the quiet cul-de-sac. I found the only place to pull over and park, which was some poor unfortunate resident's driveway.

"Morgan!" Felicity shouted and waved me over before I closed my car door.

I felt it best to make my way to her. Through a half dozen media, who somehow made it through security, and a bunch of officers milling about, I pushed my way toward Felicity. She was waiting for me off to the side of the main entryway of a home.

"When you called, you said this was our guy. Are you sure?" I asked, appearing generally puzzled.

"I know. I know I said this was the guy, and this whole thing seems different," Felicity said excitedly. "Home invasions aren't exactly this guy's bag, I get it. Wait a moment. Let me show you."

Felicity escorted me into the home, past another two or three officers taking photographs of the scene. It looked as if someone put strawberries into a blender and hit puree. It's shaping up to be on the level of our guy here.

"Through here!" Felicity called as she moved down a hallway and took a right turn into a room.

This place was tall and narrow. Personally, I wasn't impressed. I'd have to do an internet search later to quench my curiosity about the price. I rounded the corner into the bedroom to find a more horrendous scene than the last.

"The crime didn't take place in the living room?" I asked, donning gloves on my hands.

"I thought the same thing when I walked in. I don't know what the hell happened in there," Felicity said, vaguely glancing in the direction of the living room. "Based on what I can tell, the murder occurred here."

"So, you're telling me that that front room was a fucking art project for this clown?" I asked, raising my voice, letting my anger get the better of me.

Felicity looked up from the human goop pile that lay on the floor, slowly dripping from the bedspread above. "I hate to say yes?"

I had to take a moment to get a feel for the scene. So, our Chemical Burn Killer ends up killing someone brutally in their bedroom. He maims them horribly, desecrates the body, and what, starts his best impressionist art painting with handfuls of entrails? On the one hand, it checks out. This guy is a wack job.

"I think we found the chemical residue!" Dwayne proclaimed, bursting into the room.

"Jesus, D, you scared the shit out of me!" Felicity yelled out.

"Sorry! Hey, Morgan, care to come with? It's just out back near the small storage unit for the condo," Dwayne said as he motioned for me to follow.

"Felicity, I'll be back in a minute. Grab me if you find anything wild."

Felicity looked around the room, waving her hand around it to demonstrate that it doesn't get any wilder than what we've walked into. I smiled awkwardly before following Dwayne to the back. The rear entrance had no signs of forced entry. Come to think of it, the front didn't either. I was piecing the scene together in my head as we moved through to the backyard. Calling it a backyard was an overstatement. A small plot of dirt with a slab of concrete summed it up. Eyeballing it, this person had enough space to put out a single folding chair to entertain guests before feeling crowded.

"Over here!" Dwayne said, grabbing my attention back.

He tucked into a small space located under the back stairs. This door was covered in gobs of cruor in the otherwise unremarkable backyard. The outside air must have dried this area faster than the inside of the house. I noted that in my head as I looked at what Dwayne was showing me. Another vat of this human melting compound. I didn't understand the need to mutilate the victim, only to boil them down to an inedible stew. All of this made no sense. Then again, the guy following the Dahmer case probably had similar questions. I turned to get more space and gather my thoughts when a flashbulb went off.

"Shit, come on," the voice behind the fence said.

I quickly drew my sidearm. "Come out with your hands up where I can see them!"

The man moved his hands above the fence line, cell phone still in hand. I looked at Dwayne and motioned for him to grab the gate and alert the officers.

"Listen. I wasn't trying to hurt anyone. I just needed a picture, okay?" the man stuttered out in his terrified state.

A young man, possibly late twenties or early thirties, stepped out from behind the gate and into view. He was clean, well kept, and didn't fit the description of a guy who just maimed a body. I wasn't taking my chances.

"Identification. Now!" I demanded, gun still trained on him.

He slowly reached his free hand into his pocket, retrieving a dirty, worn brown wallet. He tossed it down at my feet before placing his hands in the air. I used my foot to pry open the wallet. Inside were several credit cards and a small collection of pictures of this guy and some young lady. I kept the gun trained on the kid as I slowly knelt down to view the ID card.

Jasper Marks. This asshole wasn't even from around Parkside, let alone Michigan. Some east coast paparazzo that thinks he can continue his sensationalistic bullshit. He just walked right into the wrong backyard.

"Jasper Marks? You're under arrest for trespassing on a closed crime scene investigation," I said, looking at two officers that Dwayne acquiesced for me.

The first officer turned Marks around and violently snapped cuffs on him while reading his rights. I only wished they'd have been more aggressive. This dickbag has been making my life harder than it should have been lately. Marks turned to look at me as if he had one last-ditch chance to get off the hook.

"My boss is going to kill me!"

"Get him out of my sight!" I said after the stupid, empty remark.

The two officers escorted him to the front of the house through the backdoor. I only wished they didn't parade him through the home. I wasn't sure how much he had seen or what he knew. He seemed to know a lot, based on his article. I regrouped with Dwayne.

"So, were you able to tell if it was the same compound?" I asked as I headed up the stairs toward the back door.

"I believe so. I won't know for sure until I get results from the lab, but yeah. I'm fairly certain this is our guy."

I grumbled slightly.

"You don't think it was *that* guy, do you?" Dwayne asked, looking concerned.

"No. I—well, I'm not sure. Who's to say?" I shrugged as I continued up the stairs. "We'll know a lot more once I get him to myself at the station."

Dwayne nodded and continued his work on the chemical compound. His background in chemicals and biology has really come to use in this case, to be honest. I wanted to make a point to check in with Felicity one last time before heading back to the station to pull something useful out of Marks. For the chief's sake, at the least. I rounded the hall and into the bedroom, where she collected samples to examine later at the station.

"Dwayne thinks it's for sure our guy. He found the same chemical compound." I mentioned. "This scene is a bit different, yeah?"

"How so?" Felicity asked as she dribbled red liquid into a tube.

"No half-assed work? He took care of the whole body. Last time we had limbs. The time before that, a scalp. We always found something large to go by."

Felicity frowned. "Doyle, Conners! Can you come in here, please?"

Two giant officers stormed into the room. They were gym rats, for sure. The uniforms barely fit, it seemed. Smedium was their choice size, apparently. Hell, I would too, if I was as in shape as these guys.

"Guys, can you pick up the end of the bed for me like you did earlier?"

The two officers looked at each other, showing a mild sign of disgust before complying. Each grabbed the lower leg of the bed and lifted it. I slightly crouched to get a good look. I was instantly sorry I did. Doyle shined a light onto the scene to give me a better look. The bodies of two dogs. German Shepherds, from what I can tell. And what was left of a human being. A female torso with one arm and part of a skull.

"Christ and crackers!" I exclaimed as I backed up a bit.

"That's fine. You can set the bed down. We'll move it out later to get better photos once I'm done here," Felicity said.

The two men nodded, eased down the bed, and left. I looked around the room while trying to take it all in.

"The living room?" I asked.

"Likely the dogs. We'll have DNA head to the labs to ID it back to canines. Poor pups."

I felt a lump in my throat. There was something about dealing with humans I could process. I never could deal with the death of an animal at the hands of a person. Hell, I was beside myself as a child when I overfed my hamster. Gizzy was my pride and joy. I took him to school to show off and wanted to show everyone how many carrots he could eat. It didn't go well, and it ate me up inside. Decades later, it still bothered me. That was an innocent mistake from a child. This shit was different. Some asshole consciously decided to do this. I needed to talk to Marks.

I brushed past another dozen idle officers, making my way outside to the front yard. I asked around to find out which car Marks was contained in.

"He called his boss, who put their legal team on the line. Detective, we talked for a moment, but we had nothing to hold him on," one officer finally said.

"He what?" I lost it. "He called a lawyer? And you let him walk?"

The officer held his ground. "He technically wasn't on the scene until you pulled him into the yard. He had a press pass. His boss knew his whereabouts. The lawyer explained more in detail, but I figured we had enough on our hands. I didn't want us involved in some legal debate.

"He could have been our fucking killer, dipshit!" I barked, storming off.

I fumed all the way to my car, eventually kicking the shit out of my tires in frustration for a few moments before getting inside the vehicle. I turned the car on, pulling out as erratically as possible. I was in a haze of anger and frustration. Thankfully, the car knew the way because I sure as hell didn't. I needed to get ahead of these details. I needed to get on the line with Marks' boss, his lawyers, his mother, his pastor, and anyone willing to talk to me from his end. The station was the only place I felt I could clear my head. I finished the last of my Redbull and left the gated community.

{ **16** }

Chapter 16

As I slunk back to Apex Fusion, I mentally kicked myself for being such a rookie. At this point in their career, who gets picked up by the police? Especially a police force as rag-tag as Parkside's finest. With a killer on the loose, displaying on the regular his grotesque work like its modern art, one would think the Feds or the local police would've nabbed this guy already.

My phone rang. It was one of three people. I braced myself for the inevitable and answered the fifth ring.

"Marks!" Griffin shouted in my ear. "What the hell was that? Are you trying to get pulled off this story? Do you want to be sidelined and locked up? Don't you think for a second I'm gonna cover your ass with another stunt like that!"

"I wouldn't dream of it, sir," I said. "But let me explain —"

"I hope you've got pictures," Griffin cut me off.

"That's what — I do," I said. "And let me assure you I'll be sure to bring Patti along next time."

"You two finish up. But Marks, don't get in too deep."

After hanging up, I knew I had to avoid getting my ass handed to me again by Griffin. That's if I intended to stick with this story with or without the Sentry's or Griffin's seal of approval.

Then there was that gruff, hard-boiled detective who I assumed was Morgan. He didn't state his name, but I concluded from his paunch and how he carried himself that he must've been the guy to give a wide berth to. Yet another tick in the things to avoid column of my proverbial t-chart. Somehow, though, I still feared Griffin over Morgan. Maybe it was because Morgan didn't confiscate my photographs, or perhaps I didn't know better. Still, I thought it best to avoid further contact with the lead detective on the Disfigurer case.

With the police lights still flashing on the streets behind me, I slipped into the darkness of Apex Fusion. A song, possibly the same song, ended and Becca and Patti spotted me just as I sat down. They glistened with sweat under the dim lights and came toward me, Patti in the lead, grinning.

Becca laughed as she straightened her skirt. "That was the most fun I've had in a long time. Oh my God. I'm a mess. Let me freshen up."

Patti sat beside me and nudged me in the rib. "Did you get the story?"

I stiffened at this remark. "What story?"

"I saw you slip out," Patti said. "But don't worry, Becca didn't notice."

She stood. "I'm going to freshen up, too. Catch ya later, tiger."

I turned. "What did you call me?"

But Patti was already too far away.

The evening ended soon after, with the three of us sharing a Lyft back to our places. Becca and Patti made plans for the next night during the ride while I processed the evening.

Both the note and Patti referred to me by a pet name, tiger. I didn't believe in coincidences, but I also didn't think Patti had any more inside intel on our story than I did. There was also the simple fact the latest massacre happened a few blocks away from Apex Fusion. She and I needed to carve out time to work while Becca galivanted around town on her own.

Becca and I parted ways with Patti, and the evening gave way to the soothing sound of my fingers tapping away at the keyboard while Becca slept.

The Disfigurer Reveals His Secret Obsession

Sometime between 11 p.m. and 1 a.m., the dismembered bodies of two women were found by police in Waterview, a gated community of mixed residential dwellings on the north side of town.

While drinks flowed and music blared at Apex Fusion, Parkside's serial killer had his own party. While the names of the young women have yet to be released, it is clear The Disfigurer has taken his obsession to the level of grotesque artistry.

The interior walls of the townhouse were painted with the woman's blood while parts of her decorated the lawn. Another compound was found at the scene, but police are more than just a little reluctant to share any information.

In the interim, citizens and reporters should steer clear of any future crime scenes, as police are likely to suspect any lurker of foul play in the near future.

When I finished the article, I read through it and then sent it off to Griffin. I stood and stretched, only to turn and find Becca standing behind me with the morning sun silhouetting her figure.

Becca crossed her arms. "Do you have any idea what time it is?"

"Good morning to you," I said. "Breakfast?"

She turned and muttered something about the day can only get better from here.

My phone rang. It was Patti.

"Let's meet for breakfast. The three of us, okay?"

I agreed, and Patti gave me a location in the town center.

After I ended the call, I found Becca in mid-dress. "That was Patti. Are you cool with the three of us meeting for breakfast?"

"Great," Becca said without enthusiasm. "The day is totally looking up."

{ 17 }

Chapter 17

I found myself up to my elbows in paperwork. I could barely focus on my reports because my mind wandered to the fact that Jasper Marks walked away from me. That smug little sonofabitch probably skipped merrily back to his hometown with a fresh new scoop of bullshit for the paper to print. The thought of him made my skin crawl. I never understood how the press does what it does. Then again, one may wonder exactly how I do what I do. How do I do it? It used to be a team effort with my partners Jim, Jack, and Johnny. I've been flying solo for a handful of days recently. I don't think I've had a clear head as I have had in almost a decade or more. And that's coupled with the lack of sleep. All things considered: I felt great.

One of the other impediments to my progress has been the constant bombardment by the press. Every now and again, one of these pricks would squeeze their way into the station, interrogating everyone who looked like they had a badge. Just an hour ago, Felicity had to be rescued by three officers because those fiends were crawling all over her. They'll do anything for a story. Marks seemed no different. Why was he at the house? How the hell did he even know to be there? Plus, if it was gated, how did he even get in? Did he have credentials? Were they local? I had too many questions and not enough hours in the day.

"Morgan! My office! Now!" Chief shouted across the precinct, causing a pause in everyone, including the press.

I saved my work and rushed off to his office.

"Sir?"

"Sit the hell down."

I obliged, hesitating only for a brief second. I felt like I was about to get my ass chewed off again.

"Morgan, I'll level with you. I sat here all night thinking. I listened to the prattle of those damn leeches buzzing around the outside of the building for a story," Chief Whittaker said.

I wanted to tell him that leeches don't buzz around or fly, but that was not worth the discussion or argument.

"And?" I asked, wanting to know where things were going.

Whittaker sat down in his chair and faced me head-on. His gaze was stern and severe as if he had just gotten a royal flush in the World Series of Poker. I couldn't quite read where he was getting at.

"I think I know who's behind the murders," Whittaker started. "It's a hunch, but a damn good one."

"Ok, I'll bite. Who are you thinking?"

Chief sat back in his chair, placing both index fingers to his lips while clasping his hands together.

"He's always there. He knows every intricate detail of the crimes, down to the fine details. At first, I was sure I had a mole. A leak in my immaculate ship. That still may be, but I'd like you to go with me on this one, Morgan.

"Ok, shoot," I said, wanting to get to the chase so I could get back to my mundane reports.

"It all boils down to one guy. Jasper Marks," Chief said confidently.

The way Whittaker said it made it sound as if he had caught him red-handed in the billiard room with the monkey wrench. As much as I wanted to put out on APB to grab Marks, we needed to be smart about it.

"Are you sure? I saw the guy. He's a little shaky, but overall doesn't seem to be a killer," I said, playing devil's advocate.

"Again, I'm not sure," Whittaker stood up. "I want you to do what it takes to figure this guy out. Learn about him. Get ahold of his paper. Talk to family. Whatever we need to do. I need to know about the guy."

I stood up. "I'll do what I can, sir."

I started to make my way toward the door before Chief stopped me.

"Morgan?"

"Yes, Chief?"

"I'm too old for this shit. I shouldn't have to see two mass murders in my hometown in my lifetime. Can I get your focus?"

"Sure thing, sir."

I closed the door behind me and walked to my desk. I could see how as chief, he'd be a bit rattled knowing his guy is getting away. I was sure the media wasn't helping defer any of the pressure. I sat down and stared at the blinking cursor waiting for my input. Before getting called away, I was rehashing details regarding my encounter with Marks, if only briefly. Oddly, I was called in to discuss the very subject I was typing. Putting my fingers back on the keyboard, I recalled my interesting yet brief encounter with our possible murderer.

As I plugged away at the final details regarding Marks's release from detainment, my phone rang. I answered, seeing that it was Zahra on the other end.

"Hey," I said as I answered.

"Hey yourself," Zahra quipped. "Don't you usually answer your phone as if every call was a work call?"

I shifted my phone to the other ear. "I'm trying something new. What's up?"

Zahra paused. "We're still on for dinner tonight, yeah?"

"Of course! Why the heck would I bail on that?"

"Well, I've been watching the news and seeing all of the stories from that community. Are you ok?"

I hesitated before answering Zahra. There was only so much she needed to know, and the last thing I wanted to do was have someone overhear me divulging information to someone over the phone.

"Can we talk tonight at dinner? I'll answer any question you have on the way there," I asked, hoping to move past the case.

"Sure. I understand. Is 7 PM still ok for you?" Zahra asked.

I looked at my watch to check the time. "Isn't that a bit late to take the kiddos out?"

Zahra laughed. "Yeah, it is. I hired a sitter for tonight."

I smiled a bit. I thought this was a family outing, at best. This was a *date* date. The real deal. At least, it was in my mind.

"Ok, we'll talk tonight. Pick you up at the house?" I asked.

"You got it. See you tonight," Zahra said, ending the call.

We didn't end with the traditional I love you's that we would have uttered in the past. I heard the tone Zahra spoke in. She wanted to say it. It gave me hope. Honestly, I think the sudden explosion of work has pushed me to be better. I reached down and slid open my bottom desk drawer. I shoved past the hanging file folders, reaching for the bottle I had stashed behind them. I stood, concealing it in my jacket as I made my way to the men's room. This would be my last order of business before checking out today and grabbing a quick nap before tonight. I watched twenty-seven dollars of booze go down the drain before forwarding my completed report to Whittaker.

{ **18** }

Chapter 18

My phone blew up. Not literally, of course. The Daily Sentry printed the story I caught last night, and my social media went off the fritz.

I reached for my phone.

"Again?" Becca and Patti scolded me in unison.

I stuttered over a few one-syllable words, then slid my phone into my pocket.

Becca scowled, and Patti laughed.

"Relax, Becca. Marks isn't used to all this social media stuff. It wasn't until just a few days ago that his follower count was barely three figures."

I blushed and downed the rest of my bloody Mary. We were at a cozy diner in the center of downtown Parkside, where the quaint little shops merged with the historical and the new.

Becca placed a hand on Patti's arm. "Enough talk about work. What do you say for a girl's day out?"

Patti glanced at me. "Actually... Jasper and I."

Becca rolled her eyes. "Seriously, you two. Wrap this thing up and let it rest. Don't you think the bigger papers are more capable of handling it?"

I thought about that for a moment. "I don't know. I haven't seen any other reporters on the crime scene and —"

"Isn't that just a little odd?" Becca asked.

Patti shifted her gaze between Becca and me, then back to Becca. With a grin, she said, "Your man's just good at what he does."

Becca scoffed. "Too bad it doesn't transfer to other things."

"You know I'm right here," I said, catching the waiter's attention and signaling for the check.

After paying up, I took out my credit card and handed it to Becca. "Tell you what. Give us two hours to do some digging. I'll meet you for lunch."

Becca fanned the card in front of her. "This hardly makes up for your absence, but it's a start. Where should we meet up?"

I began to offer a suggestion that was cut short by Patti. She stood, "Actually, Becca, it'll just be the two of you. If we find anything, I'll take the preliminary. If not, I'll probably pack my things and head back."

Becca raised an eyebrow. "You're sure about this?"

Patti nodded, and I clapped my hands together. "Great. It's settled. Two hours tops and I'll meet you at The Moroccan Exchange. I hear they make amazing cocktails."

I leaned in to kiss Becca on the lip, but she turned her head so I caught her cheek instead. "We'll see," Becca said. She turned to Patti. "Catch ya later."

Patti waved her off, then faced me. "You're killing me, Marks. I love a good story as much as anyone, but I wouldn't let Becca go so easily."

"I'll make it up to her tonight," I said.

Patti slapped me playfully on the arm. "You sure about that, tiger?"

I stepped away. "What's with the pet name?"

Patti shrugged. "Something my dad always said."

"Funny," I said. "Last night was the first time I heard you say it."

"Well, you must not have been listening every other time," Patti said. "C'mon. Griffin wants me to do a feature story on Parkside, and I need you to help me with a few pieces."

She grabbed her bag off the ground and swung it over her shoulder, marching off. Though I wasn't satisfied with her excuse, I was definitely curious. Especially considering this was the first time I heard about a feature story.

Our first stop was the abandoned mall on the outskirts of town. It looked as unimpressive as the pictures I saw on the news— a growth of moss overtaking the facade, windows shattered by kids likely on a dare, and a chain bolting the front door shut.

"You sure this is the place?" our driver asked.

"How about a hundred bucks to wait?" Patti asked.

The driver shrugged. "Fine by me, but I'm out of here if you're not back in half an hour."

"Deal," Patti said. She turned to me and winked before climbing out of the car.

I followed, noting the weight in the bag. "Exactly what do you have in there? Bolt cutters?"

"Protection," Patti called out without turning around. "There's another way in. I want to show you something."

Patti approached the front of the mall at an angle toward an overlap in the design of the building. I caught up with her just as we tucked ourselves behind the overlap of the wall. Immediately greeted by the stench of mold and animal feces, I choked.

"You'll get used to it," Patti said.

"Have you been here?"

Patti laughed. "What? Do you think I'm the killer?"

I forced a laugh. "No. That's ridiculous."

"Well, c'mon then. The driver isn't going to wait forever."

We came to a steel door that creaked as it swung on its hinges. Once inside what I concluded to be a maintenance hallway, Patti pulled a heavy flashlight out of her bag and switched it on. Aside from a few rats and water dripping in some distant corridor, Patt and I were alone.

I matched my pace with hers until we came to O'Hurley's, a quickly forgotten department store. Yellow police tape blocked the store entrance, but Patti ducked right under it.

I grabbed her arm. "What are you doing?"

"Relax, Marks. CSI, or whatever, hasn't been here in days." She turned into the darkness and switched her flashlight back on. "Follow if you want."

I imagined the scene would've been far more gruesome had the blood splattered from one end of the department store to the other been wet. But it was dry, and its pattern showed evidence of the absence of things. Though it was only my guess what the investigators might have moved. Perhaps mannequins or display furniture, but definitely bodies.

Still, as she snapped a few photos, my active imagination went wild. I imagined The Disfigurer slicing a woman's artery, then applying pressure as he danced her about. I didn't know whether the blood would splatter or drain out. I would need to look it up later.

Or maybe he slit the woman's throat and let it drain out in painter's buckets. Would just under a gallon and a half cover this much area? I suspected he would need at least three or four gallons to spread this much blood from one end of a department store to the other. That would take at least three hours to drain from multiple women, or forty-five minutes if he started the draining all at once.

A light flashed.

"Holy fuck!"

"What is it?" Patti called out. Her footsteps approached.

I sat, trying to slow my heart rate as I took deep breaths. "Our killer is saving up."

Something heavy and metallic clanged in the distance.

"C'mon," Patti held out her hand. "We've got to get out of here, but it sounds like this was a very fruitful trip."

Our Lyft, thankfully, waited for us. Patti delivered on the promise of a hundred bucks when our driver dropped us off at The Moroccan Exchange fifteen minutes before I promised to meet Becca.

Outside of the restaurant, I filled Patti in on my speculations. "Whatever this guy is up to, the crime scenes are only the tip of the iceberg."

Patti swiped a strand of hair over her ear. "How do you figure?"

"I'm not sure yet," I said. "But there was way too much blood at that crime scene."

Her eyes widened. "Good. Go with that. I've got to head back to the paper, but I'll make sure I send these pictures off to Griffin. I'll let him know you'll write your story, okay?"

I nodded.

She reached her hand out and took mine. "Jasper. Be careful. You *and* Becca."

I headed into the restaurant and ordered a double bourbon when we parted ways. After what I saw, I could've used three times as much but Becca had my card. After downing the first, I ordered a second, then called Becca. Her phone went to voicemail. I shot off a text to let her know I was here. Again, there was no reply. Three drinks and another hour later, I overloaded her messaging app with sad and desperate pleas to pick up the phone.

"Jasper!"

I looked up to see Becca, face flushed and hair tangled.

I stood, then thought better of it when I had to steady myself. She met me at the bar.

"Sorry, I stopped over at the bed and breakfast to drop off my things. Don't worry." Becca sat next to me and rolled her eyes. "I didn't go crazy. Anyway, this guy started talking to me. Then I realized I had lost my phone somewhere between the store and the house. So, I hope you weren't too worried."

I thought of Patti's warning for us both to be careful. "I wasn't worried."

"That's doubtful," Becca said. "How about we grab lunch, then hit the town?"

My phone chimed, drawing mine and Becca's attention to it. I picked up the phone to see a message with a photo attachment from Becca.

"What's this?" I swiped up, and Becca leaned in.

When I unlocked the phone, a picture of Becca running down a flight of stairs at the B&B popped up on my screen.

"What the hell?" Becca said with concern, snatching the phone from me. She pinched the screen and zoomed in. "This was taken within minutes of that guy I ran into. Do you think he could've stolen my phone?"

My heart sank with suspicion, but I tried to play it off. "Doubtful. We should probably order lunch, then head out."

"Whatever you say," Becca said, then handed me back the phone.

I hailed the bartender and let him know we were ready to be seated at a table. Before long, a waitress escorted us to our table.

On the way, I snuck another peek at the phone. Another text came through. If you liked your little trip to the mall, you're gonna love what comes next. But the girl will have to go.

Becca nudged me. "Who are you talking to?"

"Patti," I said, then swiped to her contact information.

The waitress paused at a table. "Here we are."

As we sat, Becca eyed me. The menus were then placed before us and the waitress asked, "What'll you folks be drinking today?"

"Iced water is fine for both of us," Becca said without looking up.

When the waitress left, Becca added, "Jasper, if you keep fixating on this story, I'm not going to be around to see it to the end."

I raised my hands in mock surrender. "I'm all yours. The phone's going away."

Just as I slipped the phone into my pocket, it buzzed. Another message awaited me, of that, I was sure. But I made a promise, one I knew I'd have to break.

For the rest of the afternoon and late into the evening, Becca gallivanted around town, dragging me from one shop to the next. As she weighed me down with trinkets, the weight of my phone shuffling around in my pockets became ever more ominous. I lost count after the thirtieth message in the span of one hour.

Finally, the opportunity presented itself when we retired for the night. Becca slipped off her clothes and into the shower. I sat on the edge of the bed, then swiped quickly through the messages from her number. Blurring images of a woman against a dark background caught my attention. She was bound and gagged, of that, I could tell. The photos took me through a sick and fascinating montage of the killer's progression — from closeups of wrists slashed to raw fingertips scorched with burns. In one of the photographs, I made out what appeared to be a silver bone knife, coated gently with blood.

The final message read Your little field trip proved fruitful. Now there's one for me and one for you. Tonight, the warehouses smell of delightful fear. The race is on, don't delay.

The shower cut off, and I grabbed my camera bag. Becca had made an ultimatum — her or the story. With no time to delay, I slipped out of the room.

Chapter 19

I felt like an absolute schmuck. I spent the better half of my early evening hours relishing in the fact I turned in a helluva report to the chief and cleaned my apartment while riding that high. I can't recall the last time I'd touched a can of kitchen cleaner or a toilet brush. I personally was embarrassed for myself. I cleaned more muck and grime out of the bathroom than any other part of this place. How did I let myself get this down in the dumps? I hit rock bottom, bounced from that boulder, and kept toppling down. That's how.

Once I was able to finish giving the apartment a solid once over, I peered my head out of the window to catch a view of the beginning sunset. It was nice to take that sort of thing in once in a while, something I'd failed to do in the past. The little things, as they say. I grabbed a towel from my linen closet, which had previously been overflowing with newly acquired booze, and stepped into the shower. I had a hot date tonight, and I didn't want to disappoint. Who was this guy? Is this really the same Kurt that passed out five months ago slumped over a gallon of milk that I attempted to pour into a bowl of cereal? I recall waking up to the stench of sour milk and ruined Cheerios. Honestly had no idea how long I was passed out, to be frank. Now look at me; wide awake, bright-eyed, bushy-tailed, and all that shit.

I sent a quick text to Zahra to let her know I was on my way before starting the journey to her restaurant of choice, Ivensons. It was a quaint little steakhouse with an upscale atmosphere. In the parking lot, I triple-checked myself to ensure I didn't have a thing out of place. I still felt like a schmuck, though. I don't think I felt this clean or looked this nice in ages. Heck, I even shaved that haphazardly grown stubble that I had amassed on my face. My beard was a close cut, five o'clock shadow style that gave me a dashing, daring, yet cozy look. Or so I thought, at least.

"Yes, sir? How may I help you?" The maître d' asked.

"Oh, yes. I'm meeting my—meeting someone here. I have a reservation under Morgan," I replied.

The server glanced down while adjusting his glasses a bit. They still used an old-school pen and paper with a fancy planner setup. Hell, I'd been in an Olive Garden, and they flashed a fancy iPod with my name on it to seat me. Maybe it was less tacky to use the pen and pad setup.

"Yes, I have you, sir. Kurtis Morgan?"

"That is me."

"Excellent," the maître d' said with a slight arrogance in his tone for no reason. "Your guest has already joined us. Right this way."

I followed the pompous prick right to the far end of the restaurant. It was a two-person booth, tucked away, nearly isolated. Zahra and I liked it because we felt cut off from the rest of the noise of this place. This was "our" booth. We weaved and dodged waiters and patrons as they moved about the dining floor. I saw the booth; with the most beautiful woman I'd ever seen waiting for me. I paused briefly, taking the moment in. She didn't do anything special, mind you. She was sipping on a glass of water, likely browsing through her phone at mindless content. She was ravishing. Her deep red berry-colored dress contoured her just right, showing off every asset she owned, yet, remained classy enough to be modest. I stumbled slightly as I made my way to the table as if this was my first time seeing this woman.

"You look great, Kurt!" Zahra said as she noticed me approaching.

"I think you look entirely too good for me. Look at you!" I stammered to say.

I took my seat as they grabbed my drink order. I ordered us the house wine, our drink of choice back in the day.

"How is work?" Zahra asked.

I hesitated for a moment. I could tell my face immediately displayed an expression of dismay. "The usual."

Zahra took a long sip of her water. "Oh, sorry. Just making conversation."

"I know you don't feel like going down that rabbit hole with work. It's the same shit, different day. You know the deal," I tried to say without seeming off-putting. "How are the kids?"

The waiter brought over our wine, displaying the bottle to us before popping the cork. We never purchased by the glass. I always wanted a bottle, fresh. As he poured, both of us remained quiet. I decided to take the time to look into her beautiful amber-colored eyes. Something about her eyes always got me. They were a soft, gentle glowing golden brown when she was happy. When she was upset, they faded to a washed-out rust color. I could tell she was having a good time tonight by her gorgeous eyes alone.

"Oh, the kids?" Zahra responded as the waiter left, leaving the bottle. "They're doing just great. Alisa started a new movie, finally."

I finished my sip of wine. "Oh, really? It's about damn time, right?"

"She's working on Frozen 2 now."

I smiled. "Well, I guess there are worse things out there."

Zahra chuckled at my awful joke. "I guess so."

I stared down at my wine for a moment. I wasn't enjoying the taste as much as I typically did.

"So, what's with," I gestured with my finger toward the room.

Zahra laughed. "You know I love their Pasta al Forno! I swore I'd never be able to come here without you."

"So, you found a loophole, it seems," I said, smiling.

Zahra returned a grin before taking a sip of her wine. I grabbed my glass and took a sip. The taste was bitter. I used to drink bottles of this stuff, yet I could barely swallow any today. I forced the gulp down my throat before flagging our waiter down.

"Ah, yes. What can I get for you?" the waiter asked.

"Well, I think she will be having the Pasta al Forno, light garlic. I'll be having the house chicken special, with goat cheese substituted for Parmigiano, like this dish has," I pointed to another dish on the menu as an example. "Oh, and can I also get a Pepsi?"

The waiter paused for a moment before replying. "Excellent choices. I'll have your beverage in a moment, and your orders will be out shortly."

I watched the waiter turn and leave, returning my gaze to Zahra.

"Well, that's different of you."

"Well, they didn't have Coke."

"That's not what I meant. I can see a difference in you, Kurt. Have you had a drink in a while?"

I thought for a few moments about it. Truth be told, I hadn't touched the bottle in what felt like years. It had been almost three weeks, by my recollection. Honestly, if I'm thinking seriously about it, it's been since this case sprung up.

"I'm just saying, you look great," Zahra added, as the waiter dropped off my soda.

I felt myself start to blush. I can't recall a time I'd last felt embarrassed or coy. Possibly grade school.

"Well, thanks. This case has been running me ragged, so that means a lot. I assumed I looked like hammered shit," I replied, trying to dismiss her compliments.

Zahra adjusted herself in her chair a bit, scooting closer to me. "No, I'm serious. You look well. After, you know. Well, you just kinda fell apart, is all I'm saying."

"I get it. Between Coombs, the Cross-Country Killer Couple, and among many other things, I broke. For that, I'm sorry."

Zahra finished her sip of wine. "I've never heard you apologize before, Kurt."

"It's a new thing I'm trying out. It's called 'being human.' I hear it's all the rage."

Our food arrived just in time. I barely recalled placing my order as we were so caught up in conversation. The elation I was feeling was written on my face. I was feeling great. I had my apartment together and clean, I was together and clean, and this date was going well. Honestly, there wasn't a thing that could shit on my parade. That is until the phone began to buzz in my chest pocket.

I withdrew my phone to silence it before Zahra spoke up. "Do you have to take that?"

I gave a halfhearted smirk as if knowing taking this call from work would be detrimental to the night. I excused myself and stepped into the restroom vestibule area.

"Morgan."

"Thank god. I wanted to get to you first before Chief did," Felicity said intensely.

"What's going on?"

"Remember your pal, Jasper? That reporter guy?"

"Yeah, what about him? I think I put the fear of God into that man last time we met. Something come up?" I asked, switching my phone to the other ear.

Felicity took a dramatic pause before speaking. "He's been caught snooping around at crime scenes. Some of our overwatch team who's been on duty have been able to positively identify him. He was with a few people, some ladies, over at the department store. They think the gate guard has been able to identify him returning again."

"Christ. This is big," I said as I ran my hand through my hair.

"I know you're on your date. I think we can send officers to get him, but that will take a bit to scramble. You're closer to his latest location, and I figured you'd want first dibs."

Felicity knew me well. Of course, I'd want to be the one to look this dickweed in the eyes as I slapped the cuffs on him. If I could throw the book any harder at him, I'd want to. I want to ruin his life. The fucking press thinks they are untouchable, and it frankly irks me to my core. They would show up everywhere after Coombs' death. I couldn't take a shit in private without someone with a recorder asking me if I had any new leads on the already cold case of mine. I had to make an example of Marks. If I could bring in his whole paper, I would.

"I'm on it. I'll take care of it. Thanks, Felicity," I said, hanging up the phone abruptly.

I weighed out how I would tell my beautiful date that I had to cut it short. I played a million scenarios over in my head about what I would say that wouldn't make me sound like an absolute asshole. I had gained so much. Another reason to kick Marks in the teeth if my progress had been for nothing.

"Do you need to leave?" Zahra asked.

I hadn't prepped for the scenario where she asks if I'm leaving.

"Unfortunately. Remember that guy Marks I told you about?"

"Yeah? What about?"

"They caught him creeping around old crime scenes. Had some women with him or something, I dunno."

Zahra finished the rest of her wine in the glass. "Go. It's fine. You need to get this guy off the street if he's the weirdo you say he is. We'll talk about this tomorrow?"

"You bet. I'm so sorry," I leaned in and kissed Zahra on the cheek. It was very forward of me, but I rolled the dice.

"Be careful," she added before I stepped away.

I quickly swiveled around back to the table, reaching for my wallet. I slapped my card down in front of Zahra. "I'd be a rude gentleman if I didn't treat you, right? I'll get this from you tomorrow."

I didn't give her a second to refute my offer. I made for the door, rushing to get to the latest scene Marks revisited: the warehouse.

{ **20** }

Chapter 20

Heavy night air clung to my skin as I arrived at the warehouses located on the outskirts of town. When we entered Parkside a few days ago, I imagined the ancient industrial complex as the skeletal remains of a thriving industry long since extinct before the mall ever showed up. The lake gurgled in an unseen but near distance just beyond one of the warehouses. Cars and trucks zoomed above where the overpass divided this cluster of buildings.

I wandered from one warehouse to another. I kept one ear trained on the police scanner and listened with anticipation for a siren coming from the traffic just above us. After entering and scanning two warehouses, I determined the unlikelihood of anything within the building. The Disfigurer's tactics had become increasingly more visible as if he taunted the authorities. Still, reverting to a dark alleyway or an abandoned warehouse didn't fit with the pattern of the last few killings. His latest work, perhaps his masterpiece, would have to be on display for all to see and at just the right time.

"The highway!" I said aloud. "He'd want to stop traffic."

I circled back around the buildings. The overpass loomed overhead, yards away from the side of the building. Thousands of drivers immersed in the routine of their daily commute couldn't miss a display if they wanted to.

I flipped my light on. A rat scurried away into the shadows and then kerplunked into the lake. I targeted the exterior wall, raising the circle of light higher until it froze on the thing — the woman, rather. Her arms were spread out and strapped to the building in classic crucifix style.

For some reason, the Disfigurer wanted me to see this new stage of work, and I'm damn sure going to do it right. I quickly set up a couple of tripods, mounting and positioning two LED lights. I had to get the angle just right to capture my — *his* work in all its grotesque beauty.

I focused my shot and snapped a few photos. As I checked them, I felt the tell-tale tingle at the back of my neck — a slight itch that needed scratching. Still, I glanced around. Someone was watching me, and I needed to work faster.

Each shot had to capture the very essence of the Disfigurer's work with meticulous care. I zoomed in on the dissolving skeletal remains of the woman's face. Whisps of short, platinum blonde hair danced on the faceless head of the latest victim. Bile caught in my throat. I swallowed it down. There'd be time to process all of this later.

Sirens blared in the distance, confirming that someone had indeed been watching us. It didn't matter. I still needed a few more shots. I scanned the warehouses around me. There had to be enough time to get a better angle.

Sirens resounded, and blue and red lights flickered in the night, indicating they were near as ever. I grabbed my things and scurried toward the car in a vain attempt to slip away.

Two police cruisers sped past me, and another three halted and skidded their tires on loose gravel. I fumbled with the camera. Blinding white flickered on. The jig, I realized, was up.

With the command to put my hands up, the rest happened quickly. I dropped to my knees as officers exited their vehicles. Then I was cuffed and pushed along into the backseat of the cruiser.

The door slammed with a resounding thud. With all those photos I took, a story of a lifetime began churning in my mind, stringing word to word and sentence to sentence. I needed a computer. More importantly, I needed to meet the Disfigurer face-to-face.

The front door opened. A uniformed officer in blue took his seat and fastened his seatbelt. He adjusted his mirror and our eyes locked.

"What're you grinning about?"

I averted my eyes, and the cruiser pulled away. As we turned onto the overpass, I caught a glimpse of The Disfigurer's latest victim. Capote's grand masterpiece was called *In Cold Blood.* My masterpiece would need an equally memorable title.

Chemical Burns came to mind. I smirked. That would do just nicely.

Chapter 21

"What do you mean you already took him in?" I barked at the beat cop, who remained vigilant on guard to watch the site.

"Look, Detective. I called it in, and things just moved faster than I expected. He's been removed at least twenty minutes, so there's a good chance nobody has had a chance to talk to him," the officer responded.

I weighed it out for a moment. I could look around and figure out just why Marks was poking his head around the scene again, or I could just ask him. I glanced at the name on the officer's chest plate.

"Thanks, O'Malley."

He gave me a nod and returned back to his vehicle, set to stare mindlessly into the darkness for another several hours. I figured I could call the station and delay anything from moving forward without my say-so. As if the universe was sending me a sign, my phone began to ring.

"Morgan."

"Morgan! Get down here right away! We got Jasper Marks. He's cooling off right now, waiting for you," Chief said, almost proud of what he was saying.

"I'm on the way, Chief. I'm leaving the warehouse he was poking around in right now. Be there in twenty," I said as the chief hung the phone up before finishing my statement.

I rushed over as fast as I could. I don't think we'd ever get a better lead than what landed in my lap here. My phone reverberated in my center console once more. I quickly pulled it up while at a red light and checked. It was Zahra.

"Hey!"

"Hey yourself. Is everything ok, Kurt?" Zahra asked with concern in her voice.

I set the phone to speaker mode and resumed driving. "Yeah, actually. They have that reporter character detained right now, and I'm about to lay into him."

Zahra was silent for a moment.

"How was the rest of dinner? Sorry about taking off so quickly," I said, breaking the silence.

"Oh, it's fine. I know the drill at this point. I'm just tired. I figured I'd give you a buzz before I went to bed, make sure things were fine."

"I'll touch back with you once I get through with Marks," I said, pulling up to the station. "I'll pop by tomorrow?"

"That works. Catch you tomorrow. Goodnight!"

"Goodnight, Zahra."

The walk into the station was daunting. I was looking forward to a lovely evening, but I suppose breaking my foot off in this reporter's ass would suffice as a viable substitute. I entered the station, which was void of the typical daytime hustle and bustle. There was an eerie hush to the building late at night. I was still dressed in my dinner clothing, too. I glanced down, noticing I wasn't quite the image of a "rugged cop" but more of the next contestant on The Bachelor. I removed my tie, loosened up my collar, and moved toward the interrogation room.

Sure enough, through the glass, I could see Marks. He looked distraught as if something was eating away at him. I was set on finding out just what that was exactly. Wasting no time, I pushed into the room and sat abruptly in the chair opposite him, staring into his eyes for a moment. I wanted to see if I could gauge his character. I have a thing about people I make eye contact with. You can learn quite a lot in the first few seconds once your gaze is locked. Is the person nervous? Are they confident? Are they a liar? You can pick a lot up in a short time.

"Remember me, Jasper?" I said, breaking the silence.

"I think so. Were you the officer who had me removed from the private residence?" Jasper replied, seeming to have a frog in his throat, which he cleared excessively.

"You're goddamn right I am. That would also be Detective Morgan to you, buddy." I decided to set things right from the start. "Why am I hearing that you're creeping around the old crime scenes? Sicko like you wants to relive the moment. Is that it?"

Jasper seemed jarred by my "cutting the bullshit" method of questioning. "I, uhh..."

"'I, uhh what?' Gonna relive the glory moments? Recall the screams? Reminisce on the smells and how it felt? Gonna pull your little dick out and give it a good flogging for old-time's sake? Is that it?"

I laid it on heavy and hard. I wasn't playing with this prick.

"Oh, God, no!" Marks said, finally speaking with his man voice. "Can I explain? Give me just a second to tell my side?"

"Sure. You got five minutes to wow me," I said, relaxing back into my chair.

I was ready for whatever cockamamie tale this asshat was prepared to spin.

Chapter 22

I took a deep breath. Morgan would want to know how I'd managed to arrive on the scene before the police arrived. Especially this last one.

Morgan crossed his arms and glared. He was getting impatient, and the clock was ticking.

"Let's start with the mall, okay?" I said. "That wasn't my idea. That was Patti Pruitt's idea. She's been assigned to work with me on the story. You can call The Daily Sentry and ask for Griffin. He'll confirm the assignment!"

"We'll do that," Morgan said. "Did you and Ms. Pruitt learn anything new?"

He was fishing, and I knew my conclusions about the blood coming from more than one woman would raise more questions. I went with a partial truth. "Nothing the police didn't already know."

"Cute," Morgan said as he sat, aggressively brushing his arms across the desk. "What do you think the police already know?"

"Seeing that I'm an investigative journalist and not a cop, I don't have the foggiest idea. But I can tell you I follow every lead. Revisiting a crime scene the police are finished with is not illegal."

"No, it isn't. Unfortunately for you, an active crime scene is a problem, and I can nail you and Ms. Pruitt on trespassing." Morgan took out a pen and pad.

I raised my hands in surrender. "Alright. The old crime scene gave me perspective. You can say it helped me get into The Disfigurer's head."

Morgan snorted. He rubbed at the bridge of his nose in frustration.

I continued. "He's passionate about his work and believes himself to be an artist, but he's tired of his work going unnoticed. As I said, nothing the police wouldn't have already concluded."

"Okay smart ass," Morgan said. "Tell me about the private residence. That was a gated community with limited access. Hell, I even had a hard time getting in myself. Some of my officers say you were already there when they arrived."

"I happened to be in the area. Patti and Becca can confirm my presence at Apex Fusion."

Morgan slammed his fist on the table. "Those bodies were mutilated hours before you were there! Same with tonight. And you and I both know your career has been less than sensational as of late. When's the last time you wrote a hit? Huh?" Morgan tapped his thumbs rapidly against the table, trying to unnerve me. "Just a has-been. For that matter, you gotta be someone before you can be a has-been. A fucking nobody is what you are. Quit holding out and tell me what I want!"

I knew what he was doing, but I wasn't going to bite. "You know you have no basis for holding me. And Patti and I can both confirm my whereabouts."

"Help me out, then Marks," Morgan said, calming himself down a bit. He pulled out a folder, opened it, and laid my stories in sequential order in front of me. "You're either really lucky, or you're obtaining the content of your articles in some repugnant, deplorable methodology I'd love to get my hands on. Even the best news agencies report on details after our press releases and fact release. You're calling this before we go public!"

"Do you really think the pattern is that difficult to predict?" I asked. "Any true crime enthusiast would be able to make a fairly accurate guess about where The Disfigurer would strike next. He's getting bolder and possibly more impatient. That's for sure."

"Let's say you are that good, hypothetically speaking," Morgan said. "It would mean you either; know the asshole, work for the asshole, or are the asshole. Which is it? Give up your source, and I'll rule out two of the three."

I realized I had already said too much, so I went with the truth. "You know it would be illegal for you to coerce me into revealing those sources."

Morgan applauded slowly. "And without a lawyer, no less."

"Only the guilty require a lawyer," I said.

"How about we cut to the chase," Morgan said. "I can charge you with two counts of trespassing. One for the mall and another for the warehouses. I can throw in obstruction and anything else I can toss in your direction. Witnesses abound can finger you at the crime scenes both while we were investigating and after we'd wrapped."

"The mall and the warehouses were abandoned," I said. "You know those charges wouldn't stick."

"Perhaps not, but you'll be out of my way," Morgan said.

He was right. I knew he could hold me overnight, and I'd lose precious time fighting it in court. Morgan stood and gathered up my old news stories.

"Wait," I said. Morgan paused and shot me a smug look. I'd let him have the victory for now. "I'd rather have the police as a friend than an enemy. Let's say we work together."

Morgan laughed. "I don't need any fucking friends, buddy."

"I have a suspicion about my initial source," I said.

Morgan narrowed his eyes. "Your initial source? You have my attention. Go on."

"He went by Mike, and he said he was with Parkside Police." I offered my hand to shake on our exchange.

Morgan hesitated before he took it. His expression blanked as he looked me in the eyes. "Stay in town. If you come across anything, you report it to me."

"Deal."

He released my hand after a final squeeze for dominance, and soon I was gathering my things and headed out the door.

The morning sun was already rising when I turned on my phone. It pinged with multiple message notifications — one from Patti, one from The Daily Sentry, and five from Becca. Becca didn't bother to text, which meant she was pissed. It also meant I'd get a hold of her first.

I ignored the voicemails. The phone barely rang once before it picked up.

"What the hell, Jasper!" Becca shouted. "I've been calling you all morning. Did you even sleep last night?"

"I've been —"

"Forget I asked. I thought this trip to Parkside would be a romantic getaway. Hell! I should've been pissed when I found out the trip was about you following a lead. But I wasn't. Then when Patti headed out, I figured you'd be wrapping up, too."

"There's been a development," I said. "The police are involved, and —"

"I don't care," Becca said. "I'm already packed and waiting for a ride to the airport. I realize now that the story will always come first. Don't bother to look me up when you get back in town."

The phone went dead, and I'd be lying if I didn't feel partial relief. Becca made the decision that I wasn't willing to make. Next, I called The Daily Sentry.

"Marks," Griffin said. "Tell me you got something."

"I do, sir. Last night's crime scene was gruesome, and I managed to get a few unadulterated photos before the police arrived."

"Well, hallelujah, and all that jazz," Griffin said. "Tell me about the scene."

I described the scene in detail, telling him I even got several close-ups. "But I have to warn you, they may be too graphic to print."

"I'll be the judge of that," Griffin said. "Get me something by this afternoon."

I found my car in the impound lot behind the police station, then I tossed my equipment in the backseat. When I arrived at the bed and breakfast, I wasn't even surprised when the manager gave me until the afternoon to clear out. He told me how my "lady friend" left in a rage, and that he didn't want that type of behavior in this establishment.

Hastily, I agreed, then headed to my room. Once there, I sat on the bed and opened my camera bag. I had taken multiple photos last night, and I needed to send these off first. I pulled the camera out, then fired up my computer. As my computer started, I popped open the media drive on the camera. The micro disk was missing. I snatched the bag off the bed, then dumped out its contents, even turning the bag inside out.

I cursed. Morgan, or someone at the station, must've kept the micro disk. I wasn't surprised when I discovered the few photos I'd taken with my phone had also been wiped. Morgan had played me, and I knew I'd have to play by his rules if I wanted even one halfway decent photo from my collection. The rest, I safely assumed, would be considered crime scene evidence.

I called Griffin back to tell him the bad news.

"Marks! Where are the photos? I've been refreshing my email every thirty seconds. Get on it!"

"Sir, I can explain. I was arrested at the crime scene and —"

"I don't want excuses!" Griffin shouted. "I want photos so grotesque I feel faint! So gruesome they'll make me vomit — in a good way, of course. Make it happen!"

When he hung up, I knew I was up shit's creek. No sooner had I placed my phone beside me did it begin to chime with an incoming call. It was my father.

"Dad?" I said, letting my caller ID make the assumptions for me.

"Jas, how's the tip?" my father said, cutting to the chase.

I hesitated for a moment before unloading a flood of information to my dad. I told him how over my head I was, including with the local police.

"Good gravy, son. You were supposed to report on it, not become the story!"

I took a deep breath. "I know, dad. I know. You know how it goes, though."

There was a muffled conversation on the other end of the line. "Hey, Jas? Your mother is giving the look. I'd better go eat supper before I become her first victim. Stay safe, ok?"

"I'll do my best. No promises," I said before the line disconnected.

My father and I had a strange relationship. While I respected him, and he did many fatherly things, it seemed we were almost business partners. I think if Becca and I have children of our own one day, I'd like to think I'd be more personable. I daydreamed for a moment about the possibility of a future with her.

My phone buzzed with a new message. I didn't recognize the number, and my breath caught in my throat when I read the text.

> *How'd you like my little display?*

I screamed and threw the phone across the room, shattering it instantly. The stairwell pounded with footsteps, and the door to my suite opened immediately.

"I know," I said, raising my hands in surrender. "I'm leaving."

The clerk waited, one hand clutching a phone, as I repacked my camera bag and stuffed a change of clothes in the space that was left. Then I hoisted the bag over my shoulder and picked up a wad of loose clothing Becca had left for me. I assumed she had taken my suitcase and emptied it, just to spite me.

I didn't care anymore. I was done with the relationship, and I was done with the story.

Fuck this disfigurer guy.

If I was on my own, he'd have to be as well.

$$\{\ 23\ \}$$

Chapter 23

I sat at my desk, staring blankly at a spread of files, photos, and reports. Everything was jumbled and out of place. Worst of all, Marks walked. The little rat shit bastard was in my hand and squirmed his way out. He knew people in high places, or rather, the lowest of places. At best, I could have kept him for a day. What good would that do? I ripped open the lower file drawer of my desk, glancing at the empty space the booze had once been.

"Fuck!" I screamed, slamming the drawer closed.

Marks was getting the best of me. I had to play it cool, or else I'd be admitting he's winning. It's always a game with these types. They want to play little head games with you until you break or give up. I wasn't doing either. I gently composed myself and woke my computer up from sleep mode. There had to be something out there. Something useful existed; I knew it.

"Morgan! My office in five!" Chief yelled from his office doorway.

I was in zero mood to deal with anything he wanted to rip me apart about. I passed the few moments rifling through a few photos of the scene, eyewitness accounts, and a map of the locations. Nothing lined up. He wasn't targeting anything specific or anywhere in particular. There was zero fucking pattern. I almost had this psychopath figured out until Marks got his grubby little hands on some information. He shows up with all of this info. Clues I'd never seen. Things connected.

It ate at me. I'd procrastinated enough; it was time to face the music in Chief's office.

I entered the room, unsure of what I'd be greeted with. To my surprise, the chief was sitting at his desk, smiling. At first, I thought he'd lost his mind. It's cynical to think that this man would be in good spirits at the boiling point of a huge case flowing out to the public, perpetuated by Jasper Marks.

"Morgan, have a seat," Chief said, motioning to the chair opposite him. "You know what I always say?"

"You say a lot of things."

"Yeah, but the one about taking the little victories? We got one today."

I shifted uneasily in my seat. Marks walked out the door, our killer is on the loose, and this man is boasting about a victory? "And what's that, sir?"

Chief Whittaker sat forward in his chair. "I got the fucking mole. Your pal Marks wasn't entirely useless."

"Wait, what?"

"We went back through the chat you had with him. He mentioned by name who did it. A few emails and texts were reviewed, and he was outta here!"

I sat in shock. The whole conversation with Marks, I kept trying to pit everything on him. I was so blinded by the witch-hunt I was on that I glazed over the fact he gave critical information.

"Christ, you're right!" I said in realization. "He said that a Mike was his source."

"Only one Mike in our district. Polarski. He's done."

I sat back in the chair. "That really is a small victory. That was Marks' source? Who divulged all of this info?"

"It would appear so, Morgan."

I had about ten new scenarios running through my head. One of which was that Marks wasn't even the killer; rather, he was a pawn in the killer's game. Worse yet, he was just a tool and likely the next victim! I shook the thought out of my head. Doubtful Marks was the killers' type.

"Morgan, I want you to take the rest of the shift off. Go clear your head. Take the case home with you and mull it over with a marathon of Seinfeld reruns or something."

Was I in that bad of shape? Chief has dismissed me several times with this case. I suppose some sleep would be good, maybe some real food in my system.

"Ok. I'll let you know if I figure out anything," I said, standing up.

Chief said nothing as I exited the room. He returned to the Sudoku puzzle he had been working on. We all had our hobbies, I suppose. I gathered the collection of files from my desk, locked my computer, and headed to the garage. A change of scenery without interruption might be a good thing. I tossed everything in the passenger seat and dialed Zahra.

"Hello?"

"Hey, Zahra. It's me. I wanted to call once I was free."

"It's so late," Zahra paused. "It's just past three in the morning. Is everything ok?"

I started the car, placing the phone in my console. "It is. I got to get my moment with that reporter fellah."

"Oh, well, that's good. I heard your car start. Are you headed somewhere?"

"Somewhere and nowhere. I need to get away from this case for a moment to get a better handle on it if that makes sense."

There was silence on the other end for a moment. I half assumed she'd fallen back asleep.

"You can come over here if you want. I was planning on taking the kids to the zoo tomorrow. It would be great if you could come with."

I hesitated for a moment while making a left turn. "Sure. I can do that. See you in an hour?"

"I'll be asleep, but you know your way around the house."

"Ok, see you soon."

I disconnected the phone. I figured I'd already woken her up, as it were, so I better let her get back to it. I completely lost all sense of time and date. I checked my phone at the next red light, seeing it was a Saturday, damn near quarter to four. I still had a few changes of clothes at the old house, so I went straight there. No sense in swinging by the apartment first. The kids would be excited. If anything turned up, the adventure would be cut short. I can't say it isn't for lack of trying that I'm wedging my way back into normalcy.

Chapter 24

I awoke with a start and shielded my eyes from the daylight that poured through a cracked window caked with soot. After I slugged about town yesterday in a desperate attempt to drown out my failure with the story, my relationship with Becca, and the police, I somehow found my way to one of those cheap motels. As I arose out of bed, the back of my head throbbed, and my eyes locked onto a nearly empty fifth of bourbon. I staggered over to my bag with a headache, pounding with regret and excuses.

After pulling out my computer, I fired it up and then began to turn the room inside out as I searched for my phone. At the very least, I needed to check in with Becca to see how she was holding up. But I stopped my search when I realized I'd shattered it yesterday while at the bed and breakfast before the manager firmly requested I vacate the premises. Somehow, I had to force myself to check in and face Griffin and the social media followers I'd amassed in my haphazard reports about the Disfigurer.

An email came through from Griffin demanding the story and the pictures. I pounded out a shitty draft titled *The Grotesque Imitates Art with the Disfigurer's Latest Victim.* Without the images for reference, I struggled with the initial details. Eventually, I managed to recreate some semblance of the unadulterated truth, careful to paint the police in the best light, casting Detective Morgan as the jaded hero in pursuit of a devil who has been outsmarting him from the get-go. I attached the news story and intentionally left out the fact that I didn't have photographs for Griffin to drool over as he selected the most provocative to publish in the Daily Sentry.

Somehow, I needed to get into the good graces of one of Parkside's finest and obtain at least one of the photographs they'd confiscated when they picked me up last night. But first, I needed a replacement phone if I planned to get a hold of anyone.

It was early afternoon by the time I cleaned up and headed out of the motel. Main Street was thinly populated with pedestrians in suits or casual wear headed in and out of offices or shops. I noted a man on the other side of the street matching my stride. He wore dark sunglasses and a hoodie and kept his gaze to the ground. A woman wearing a pink blouse scurried toward me, and her eyes darted from one building to the next. She was laden with shopping bags and bumped into me without apology as she passed by. My parallel shadow in the hoodie didn't seem to take notice. Maybe I was paranoid in my assumption that Morgan was tracking my movements using some off-duty cop. Either way, last night's debacle revealed one thing. Even without the police, someone was following me, and they were likely hiding in plain sight, just beyond my peripheral.

After another block of near misses from inattentive pedestrians, I came to Parkside Wireless, a dealer for what appeared to be at least three major cell phone carriers. That would have to do. As I reached for the door, someone else collided with me, knocking me off balance.

Firm hands grabbed hold of me, and I made eye contact with a man.

"I'm so sorry," he said as he brushed me off. The expression in his dark brown eyes matched his words. I barely had time to offer my usual *don't worry about it* before he was off without another word.

I turned back toward the retail store and headed inside, but not without glancing over my shoulder. The hoodie guy was gone, and my suspicions of being followed went with him. A store clerk greeted me.

"This is embarrassing," I told her. "I broke my phone last night."

She nodded and smiled with feigned understanding, then showed me a selection of phones available for my carrier. The door chimed, and she excused herself to help another customer. As she did so, my pocket vibrated. I glanced around. If I were being punked, someone would indeed be watching me. The customer behind me busied himself by fidgeting with the latest smartphone while the store clerk assisted another couple. I turned away from the door and pulled from my pocket a smartphone with one message notification. I swiped to open it, and the screen promptly unlocked. I read the message.

Now that you're back on track, it's time for some real fun.

I gripped the phone tight and darted out the door. It was time to follow another hunch, and I ran down the street. That man who bumped into me couldn't have gone too far. When I rounded the corner, I paused. The town block was populated with vendors ranging from crafters to farmers, and pedestrians milled about, apparently enjoying the sights. I did a complete three-sixty turn as I scanned the crowd. My hopes of spotting the man were dashed.

Just as I had given up, my eyes locked with a uniformed officer's. I realized then that I probably looked a little suspicious. I waved at him, and he gave me a nod. Then, I mingled with the shoppers as another text came through.

Check your email and your breath. You're welcome.

Like a hooked fish, I followed my intrigue and abandoned all attempts to catch up with whoever slipped me this phone. I took off toward the motel, sidestepping pedestrians along the way until I came to the outskirts of town, where the owners required a day's payment in advance and asked no question.

{ 25 }

Chapter 25

I woke up on the couch to the sound of a screaming child.

"Daddy!" Alisa shrieked.

I sat up, rubbing my neck. I hadn't slept right in quite some time, let alone on the sofa. Looking back, I can't recall the last time I slept on this couch sober, to be honest. I looked around to see Zahra standing in the doorway. Alisa fumbled for the remote, navigating the smart system to put on the film I least expected: Frozen 2.

"No movies, Ali! Go get ready!" Zahra demanded, pointing to the upstairs.

Alisa pouted. For someone who was gearing up for a trip to see some animals, she sure as hell didn't act like it. I watched as she stormed off angrily toward her room to get dressed. I hadn't seen Davey, so I figured I'd ask.

"Davey still in bed?"

Zahra poured a cup of coffee from the recently filled pot. "He's been like this for a while. I can't get him to move sometimes. I'm worried about him, Kurt."

I stood up, stretching all of my stiff muscles. I heard several bones pop, reminding me of my age. I needed half a bottle of aspirin in my bloodstream if I wanted to make it through the day. A trip to the zoo seemed like the best way to connect with the kids and maybe even

Zahra. If I could get at least one thing to go right these days, I'll be in a better mindset to get this killer.

"I'll go up and grab Davey, I suppose," Zahra said, taking one final sip of her mug before placing it on the counter.

"No, allow me," I said, trying to do the right thing as a father. "I'll talk to him."

The door to Davey's room was slightly ajar. I could hear the sounds of a teenager thumbing through hundreds of social media posts. The silence was the dead giveaway. I didn't hear snoring, so meme surfing was likely all he was up to. I gave the door a gentle rap with my knuckle before entering.

"What?" Davey asked, not even looking up from his phone.

I called it. Surfing mindlessly. "What'cha looking at, champ?"

I moved to sit on the edge of the bed. "Everything ok?"

Davey hesitated for a moment. "Are you and mom getting back together?"

Man, this kid didn't waste time. He cut through the bullshit. I wish more adults were as direct as he was; it'd sure as hell cut my effort down in this world.

"I don't know, son. I'm trying my best to be back in your lives. I really am."

"Until something happens at work, and you become a drunk again!"

"Davey, I'm sorry. I truly am. When you're an adult, you'll see—"

"You don't think I have problems, Dad?" Davey snapped, setting his phone down on the nightstand. "I get bullied because my dad is a cop. My parents are divorced. I wear glasses. I have acne. You don't think these kids don't make my life hell?"

"Language, bud. I get it; I do. I was weak. If I could have half your courage, I wouldn't be in this mess. I didn't realize what you guys were to me, which was my strength. I screwed up, and I've apologized for it a million times."

"And how is this going to be different than any other time?" Davey asked with intensity.

I looked him in the eyes. "It will be. All I can say is I'll try. Let's start by getting ready to go to the zoo."

Davey's expression changed. "The zoo? We haven't been there in forever."

"I know. Now, go get yourself together and be downstairs in a few. Parking is a pain, and I want to get a decent spot," I said, stepping out of the room.

The zoo was a madhouse. I didn't think it would be so busy on a weekday. It felt like an eternity to get through the line. Alisa was bouncing around excitedly. We had to get to the cheetah exhibit if she was ever going to settle down. Something about those things. I don't even think we ever saw half the animals outside in their habitats, but she loved the thrill of the possibility.

"Calm down, sweetie. We'll get there. Want to hold the map and navigate?" I suggested, handing Alisa the map.

She took it without hesitation, looking it over once. She couldn't really read everything, but she knew pictures. "Africa is here, right, Daddy? Let's go!"

I checked what she was pointing at. She was such an intelligent kid. "That's right, honey. I guess we'll head there."

We moved through the Florida exhibit toward Africa. I found it odd that we had an entire zone dedicated to a state and another for a continent. Then again, I've been to Ft. Lauderdale on a business trip, and I can see why half that state belongs in a zoo. Snakes, gators, and other wildlife roam the streets freely. Meanwhile, here they all were, trapped behind glass or bars. What a world we lived in.

"Oooh! Daddy, what is that thing?" Alisa asked.

I looked at what she was pointing at. "Oh, that's a ball python. I don't know if they're really from Florida. A big ol' snake."

"Neat."

I watched her toddle off in amazement. I looked over at Zahra, who was taking photos of a very unenthusiastic Davey standing next to a nice-looking mural of the Everglades. I motioned that we were moving onward toward the African exhibit. Davey schlepped along and moved toward the exit, following his sister.

"Davey, keep an eye on her, bud," I said, reaching for my phone.

My phone had buzzed twice with a text message. I ignored the first one, trying to enjoy the moment. After the second, I assumed it was urgent. I unlocked the phone and glanced at the messages. It was from Felicity. It was a simple set of coordinates from Google, with a message that read, "Another one. I'm tied up with the lab. Officers headed to the scene."

I didn't want to drop the news to Zahra and the kids. I knew I needed to keep my promise to look at this damn wildcat before we had to leave. I closed my phone up and put it back in my pocket. Before I could say anything, Zahra had the look. I knew that look. She knew damn well I was about to jet off to another case.

"Hey, we gotta see the damn cheetah," I said.

"I figured. Another one?" Zahra asked.

I nodded. I turned my gaze toward Alisa, who was bounding down the path with Davey holding her hand. He seemed the least bit thrilled to hold her hand as if it would cramp his style more than it already had been. We didn't say much more to each other about the case, only that we mutually needed to see this cat, or we'd never hear the end of it from Alisa.

Passing by elephants, hippos, and giraffes, we beelined it to the cheetah exhibit. Alisa slammed her body as close as possible to the barrier to see into the enclosure. It was a damn miracle because I think I spotted something near some foliage. I grabbed Alisa and tossed her on my shoulders.

"Over there by the bush. See it?" I asked, pointing at the cheetah.

I could feel the elation from this kid. This was the first time this sonofabitch showed itself since we'd been going to this zoo. Hell, I don't think I've even seen one out since I was going to this zoo as a kid. Even though I would have to drop the family back off, today was a win in my book.

The drive back was anything but quiet. Alisa kept talking about the cheetah, waving the gift shop stuffed animal we picked up to demonstrate. Even Davey chimed in with his input on the critter. It was just lovely to hear everyone happy and hopeful. As I dropped them off, Zahra stepped up to the driver's side window. I rolled it down as quickly as the electronic motor would go. Without hesitation, she leaned in and kissed me on the cheek.

"Thank you for a great day, even if it was cut short."

"Yeah. I'm really sorry about that. I need this to be over," I said.

"Get this bastard off the street, okay?" she said before I drove off.

I looked in the mirror to see her and the kids waving me off. It's been so long since I'd had that level of support. It was nice. Zahra was right; I needed to get this bastard off the street. I wasn't looking forward to the latest crime scene. As I turned onto the freeway, a call came across the dispatch.

"Attention, any units in the area, please respond to a distress call at the Church of Christ off Evanwood Road."

I was fifteen minutes from there. "This is detective Morgan. I can be there in a few. I'll radio in if it's over my head."

"Copy that. Car 19 is noted as responding. Thank you, Morgan," dispatch said as I quickly turned off the next exit en route to the church.

I wouldn't have deviated from the crime scene, but what's done is done over there. I had a hunch that who or what I was looking for was at this church. It was already a great day; it only could get better.

{ 26 }

Chapter 26

As soon as my computer booted up, I checked my messages one more time. There was nothing new from the Disfigurer, so I took a seat on the edge of my bed and checked my messages. I sifted through inquiries from co-workers and found nothing, then opened one email marked urgent, sent just under ten minutes ago from Griffin.

> *I'll give you until the close of business for you to explain yourself, then I'm turning you and these over to Parkside Police.*

"What the hell?" I muttered as I realized this was a reply to an email sent from my account. I clicked on the original email, apparently from me.

Several images were attached, and I knew I should contact Parkside Police and ask for Morgan. Would a guilty person tell all? I didn't know but knowing Morgan, he'd probably think I was covering up. I didn't send these, but curiosity got the better of me.

I opened the first attachment and my breath caught in my throat. The image showed Patti bound and gagged. Her platinum blonde hair was disheveled, and her eyes were wide with fear. My heart raced, and my breathing got heavier as realization sank in.

I scrolled to the next photo, then the next, horrified and enthralled by the process. One image showed a hacksaw cutting through the veiny flesh of her wrists, while another depicted a box cutter slowly and methodically cutting into her bare torso. On and on, the photos went, each one more gruesome than the next. Tears welled up in my eyes as I imagined the terror she must have felt while this monster carefully and methodically mutilated her body. The final image depicted the worst of it — her face dissolving from a liquid substance poured directly onto her face. I would've prayed she was far too gone to have felt the pain, but I knew it was too late.

My phone rang, and my hand shook as I picked it up and brought it to my ear.

"Marks!" Griffin bellowed.

I swallowed the lump in my throat. "I've... got... nothing."

"You're damn right you don't, you fucking sicko! I just want to know one thing. Why Patti? Was it a crime of passion? Could you no longer handle that she and Becca dated in college?"

"What?"

"And I didn't even bother to look at the video. What did you do? Record it all so you can revisit your sick little hobby?"

"The video?" I repeated dumbly. "My sick little hobby?"

I scrolled to the next file, an MP4. Griffin's voice droned in my ear as the video played, fading in from black and zooming in on a lone subject bound and gagged just as Patti had been. She struggled with her restraints, and ropes rubbed her wrists raw. Then she turned and made eye contact with the camera. The video froze on her face; razor-thin blood trickles ran horizontally down her face.

I dropped the phone and vomited. Becca had already become the Disfigurer's next victim.

My phone hummed again, announcing another call. I swiped it up and ended the call from Griffin. The police, I knew, would be looking for me.

"He - Hello?"

The voice on the other end was garbled. "United Church of Christ. Don't worry, it's mostly abandoned."

"Why, Becca?" I shouted, but the call had already ended.

I slammed my computer shut and stuffed it into a satchel which I slung over my shoulder. Then I darted out of the room, leaving my equipment and vomit for the police to find later. I didn't care. Not about the story, nor about getting caught. But I needed to hold on to any evidence that I could use to prove my innocence, and I couldn't let Becca meet the same fate as Patti.

As I drove to the church, I kept my head on a swivel, constantly checking my mirrors for any tails. I spotted a pawn shop advertising that it sells gold, guns, and ammo to my right. I hit the brakes.

Before getting out, I checked my mirror. A bit of vomit hung on my chin, which I wiped off with the sleeve of my shirt. Then I ran my fingers through my hair and hoped it was enough to hide the crazed maniac I knew was ready to burst out at any moment.

The door to the pawn shop chimed, a comforting familiarity amid the chaos within and around me. The clerk at the desk stared at his phone and didn't bother to look up when I entered. He was young, in his early twenties, and sported a thickly gelled spike of black hair, eye shadow, and a ring pierced through his septum. I cleared my throat when I approached.

The clerk rolled his eyes, then gazed at me. "Are you buying or selling?"

I looked at the handguns encased in the glass display, then at the rack of rifles on the wall behind him. These would require a background check and time I didn't have.

"What do you have that doesn't require a background check?"

The clerk smirked. "Come this way."

I followed him down the counter until we came to what I recognized as replicas. Toy guns with orange tips set out on display just like the others. I spotted a name I recognized.

"The Glock G17," I said, then I looked him in the eye. "And some pellets."

As he boxed the items up, he avoided further interaction with me. He likely suspected something was up, but I hoped I didn't come off as a noob or anything. He didn't let on if I did, and only time would tell if he suspected me of anything suspicious.

I was out the door and in the car in less time than it would have taken for a background check. I tossed my purchase on the seat beside me and keyed the ignition. One neighborhood seemed to blend into another, slowly morphing until window panes turned into broken glass.

Once the church came into view, I punched the gas and squealed into the parking lot. Then I pulled out the handgun. After loading the magazine, I checked the safety and slid the gun into the small of my back. I didn't want to draw too much attention, especially not in this neighborhood.

The evening was approaching and I figured it best to slip through a backdoor, which I found ajar. I slipped through the backdoor and into the darkness, mentally kicking myself for not bothering to buy a flashlight.

{ 27 }

Chapter 27

I pondered what I'd encounter on the drive over. Would I find the Disfigurer? Would it be the unlikely secret lair of a disgusting individual, further driving this depraved fellow up the ladder of fucked up shit? A church was the last place I'd guess to discover a secret hideout or a murder shack. I'd have never pegged church on the bingo board if I was playing the game. I guess I'd find out once I parked.

The church had been decommissioned back in the 90s. The last of its use was that of a bingo hall for another handful of years, finally becoming an empty husk in the early 2000s. Pulling up to the parking lot, it was clear that its congregation hadn't said a single prayer in over twenty years. Not one old lady yelled bingo in at least fifteen. The overgrown grass told a tale of a groundskeeper who'd given up. The graffiti and glass bottles showed that the local kids and riffraff came here to likely have sex, smoke pot, or do other things I'd no less prefer to push out of my mind.

As I parked my car, I observed a completely empty parking lot. Save for another vehicle, haphazardly parked. Whomever it was, they were clearly in a hurry. I felt it best to see what I could find. By the time backup arrived, too much time would have passed, the element of surprise would be wholly lost. I needed to get inside and see what was going on. I checked my sidearm and magazine before exiting the vehicle. I moved toward the abandoned car. It was too well kept to have been here for too long. I drew my sidearm, checking the interior. Empty, as expected. I tried the door. No such luck.

I scanned around the interior as best as possible. It was a rental, that was for sure. The killer could very well be renting or have a stolen car from a renter that they killed. Possibilities rushed through my head. I moved toward the church to hopefully catch the owner of the vehicle off-guard. Part of me hoped that this was the killer, but I was not as optimistic. Ever since the Crazed Lovers killers got away from me and the death of Coombs, I haven't been lucky in ages. This was my chance to turn things around.

I moved quickly to a small side door. The grass had overgrown, which was expected for a decommissioned church. It wasn't entirely unkempt, however. I trudged through the grass, placing my body against the door frame. I gripped my pistol as I reached for the door-knob. Oddly unexpected, the knob had slack and opened with ease. I pulled out my cellphone, activating its lamp feature. It barely illuminated the dark, near windowless room. I moved inside, closing the door behind me.

"Hello? This is Detective Morgan of the Parkside PD. Is there anyone here?" I called into the darkness.

Color me shocked, but the room was empty. I panned the light around each crevice of the room. This was the office of the pastor or priest, likely for administration. I could see a dust-covered desk with what I assumed to be a stolen computer, evident by the array of cables left behind. Papers and books littered the floor and cabinets as if someone had rifled through them previously. I panned my light around the walls. I really couldn't see for shit with the light, either. I heard a noise from outside a door just ahead. I assumed it led to the main chapel. Putting away my cell phone, I moved for the door, which pushed open with ease.

I crouched down a bit, moving through the darkness. Faint light bled through the numerous stained-glass portraits on the wall. A hole in one of the Apostles allowed a significantly bright beam of light through the room. Peering around, I noticed a brilliant source of light near the altar. It was a projector, looping some video that was clearly very much out of focus. None of this bode well. I pulled the safety off, ready for whatever was aching to spring on me at a moment's notice.

I noticed a figure pass across the beam of light in the room. Before I could speak, they drew a weapon, aimed, and took a shot. I felt it strike me in the shoulder. Instincts kicked in, and I returned fire, attempting to disarm this asshole. The killer wasn't getting away from me this time. I purposely whiffed the shot, aiming to the left of center mass. It was a hit. My assailant dropped the weapon and hit the floor. I nursed my shoulder for a moment before realizing I wasn't even bleeding. Relieved, I kept my gun trained on them as I moved in.

{ **28** }

Chapter 28

I clutched my side as I rolled on the floor. My scream echoed throughout the church. The white glow of a cell phone flashlight approached, and I shielded my eyes as I turned. I could make out the bulk of a man from the other side and knew his gun was trained on me.

"Marks? Detective Morgan. Keep your hands where I can see them."

I complied and complained. "What the fuck, man? You shot me!"

"I barely grazed you," Morgan said. He kicked my rifle away. "And who brings a BB gun to a gunfight?"

"Intimidation. It's all I could get."

Morgan holstered his weapon. "It was stupid. I could've killed you."

As I rose, I clutched at the wound. It was already wet and sticky with blood. "I need to get to the hospital."

Morgan grabbed my shoulders and spun me around. He shined his flashlight upon the wound and ordered me to lift my shirt. He laughed. "It's already stopped bleeding. You'll live. I've got antiseptic and gauze in the car."

Once outside, Morgan directed me to sit on the car's hood and remove my shirt. He removed a first-aid kit from his trunk. I shed my shirt as he snapped on some gloves, pulled out a cotton wad, and doused it with antiseptic. Without warning, he pressed the gauze to my skin.

"Shit! That stings."

"Better than dead. I could get you on another count of obstruction of justice. What were you doing in the church?" He tossed the used gauze, then pressed a dry one against my skin. "Hold this for a moment."

I directed my attention to my rental, where I parked it haphazardly on the curb. The driver's side door and trunk were both open. I had been in haste and could've been ambushed at every moment. I sighed. "I was following another tip."

"A call came through about a distress call. Do you know anything about that?" Two additional vehicles pulled up, and two uniformed officers got out. Morgan turned. "I'm holding Mr. Marks for questioning. Secure the scene."

I decided to come clean. "Did you see the video playing in the church?" When Morgan didn't respond, I continued. "That's my girl-friend. He's taken Becca. She's his next victim. Listen! You can either help me or stay out of my way."

Morgan took a step back. I couldn't tell whether he was ready to arrest or detain me. Either way, he gave me a hardened look while reaching into his pocket. Then he handed me a card.

"When trouble finds you again, give me a call before you do something stupid that'll compromise this investigation or get yourself killed."

I snatched the card out of his hand. "Thanks for nothing."

Back at the car, I slam the trunk and the driver's side door to the tune of Morgan yelling something about not going too far. Muttering various insults, I tossed the card next to me and peeled out of the park-ing spot. He could've easily sent one of the cruisers after me, consider-ing by now the show of force at the church had already doubled.

The phone in my front pocket buzzed, and I fumbled with it, swerv-ing the car to the left, then to the right. Popping the phone to my ear, I answered it.

"What?!"

A distorted voice on the other end answered me. "Well, that was a cute scene between you and the detective."

"Fuck you!"

He tsked. "Touchy. Touchy. Your next location is on the corner of MLK and Central. You'll know it when you see it."

"Listen here! You don't know what—"

My voice trailed off when I realized he'd hung up. I reached for the business card beside me, and my hand came up empty. I'd been blinded by my emotions and tossed it just anywhere. As I drove on, I reached for the floor, fumbling around until my fingers caught the corner of the card.

A car horn blared, and I popped back up with Morgan's card in hand. My rental careened toward an oncoming car. I swerved left, slamming into a large tree, receiving a wallop of a punch in the face from an imploding airbag.

{ **29** }

Chapter 29

"Morgan!" a familiar voice cried out from behind me.

"Felicity, I'm glad to see you," I said, slumping against a small decorative rock arrangement outside the church. "I'm beat. This —this case. It's too much."

Felicity removed her glove to wipe sweat from her brow. "I hear ya. Did you find Marks? There's blood inside."

I shook my head. "I found him, but he's not my guy. I think he's a puppet."

"You've said that before, I think. Makes sense. Marks doesn't seem like the mastermind type."

I glanced toward the church, where two officers retrieved the old projector playing the grainy, distorted video. "What the hell was on that tape, anyhow?"

"I focused the footage on the system. Some woman. Possibly the killer's next, or rather, upcoming victim that we've yet to find?" Felicity seemed just as perplexed as I did.

"That is horrendous. I couldn't identify the video, but I had my hands full."

"You shot Marks?" Felicity asked excitedly. A bit too excitedly, if you ask me.

"I did. I grazed his arm, patched him up, and he took off. Tossed him my card since he's got some sort of inside track on this whole thing. Figured it'd be better to keep him on my side if I could. Flies with honey, as they say."

Felicity nodded. "Well, I'm not sure exactly what else you can do here. Dwayne is inside grabbing anything in that church that looks useful to our case. Chief has the rest of the day off for a dentist appointment but wants reports on his desk ASAP. You know the drill."

I did know the drill all too well, unfortunately. It's the same shit, different case. I write reports, and the killer goes free. All I have to show for it is some finely written paper, double-spaced. Other than the attaboy I expected after getting enough information to be considered "good enough," the rest of the work just felt unfinished and unsatisfied. I wasn't going to stand for that this time. I was going to get this guy, even if it meant working with that moron Marks to do so.

"I'm going to head out. I want to get myself together and get a report in sooner than later," I said to Felicity as I stood up.

"That's fair. Be safe, Morgan," Felicity said as she moved back toward the entrance of the church.

I got into my car and just sat. I didn't do anything. I closed my eyes and just sat. I needed a minute to collect myself before starting this several-ton hunk of metal down the road. I took a deep breath to calm myself, finding my center as I did—punching the steering wheel with all of my strength. I half figured I'd broken it by the sheer ricochet my hand had from it. Thankfully, they built these things to last. My hand, not so much. I let out a chain of obscenities before shaking off the pain. I had to get out there. I needed to get this guy.

My car coasted along the wood-lined road that led from the church. It was a nice area, all things considered. A park was just up the road to the right, with a brand-new shaved ice place just to its right. Aside from the defunct church, this location wasn't that bad off. To be honest, I don't even know that we've had too many reports of crime out here. I stopped at a stop sign at the end of the road. No cars were coming in either direction, of course. It would be my luck to be t-boned by some airhead not paying attention because I didn't want to stop. I continued driving the path down the road.

Up ahead, I saw smoke. Before I could call it in, the source came into view: Jasper's rental vehicle. It had been completely caught up in a giant oak tree, which clearly totaled the car. They don't make them like they used to. Too many plastic parts. Smoke billowed from the hood as I parked nearby. Quickly, I moved to the driver's seat to check on Jasper, but to my dismay, the seat was empty. That asshole abandoned his car. I decided to return to my car and search for this jackwagon.

No sooner than I started my engine did I see someone walking up ahead. This person shambled and stumbled similarly to someone who'd just been in a collision. I think I'd found Jasper. I pulled my car alongside him.

"What the hell are you doing, moron? You could have gotten someone killed!" I screamed.

He stopped shuffling along and looked at me.

"Get the fuck in the car. Now!" I ordered, motioning to the backseat.

I watched as Jasper glanced back at his car for a brief moment before opening the door.

"I hope I got the coverage," he said as he closed the door.

I rubbed my eyes for a moment. The stress and the tension in my life were at an all-time high, and now I had to babysit a man-child.

{ 30 }

Chapter 30

As I rode with Morgan through the surrounding neighborhood, my phone alerted me. I pulled it out and glanced at it quickly.

Lose the fuzz, or your woman is dead.

"What is it?" Morgan asked, a touch of concern in his voice.

"The office," I said, my fingers rapidly hammering out a reply. *"Losing him when I can. "*

Not sounding pleased with my short response, Morgan followed up, "How long have you been in contact with the killer?"

He was fishing, so I laughed bitterly. "Oh yeah, and we're just passing Becca between each other."

Another text came through while Morgan pressed the car forward, his jaw clenched. I peeked at my phone, greeted by an address of 214 Franklin Street. I choked.

"Cut the shit, Marks."

"The one hundred block of Franklin Street," I said. "He didn't say which house."

Over the next five minutes, I had plenty of time to think. The Disfigurer had evaded the police on multiple occasions, often staying miles ahead of them. As for his communication with me, he'd dropped the bait and waited for me to bite. He had to be within my vicinity, keeping a watchful eye on me. Keeping my head on a swivel, I scanned the area as we drove. As cars pulled to the right or left, nothing stood out to me.

We turned down a ghostly neighborhood of boarded-up houses and cracked pavement.

"Keep an eye out," Morgan said as he scanned the neighborhood street.

"Up ahead," I said and pointed as if I knew where we were going.

When the car came to a stop, Morgan was the first to climb out. "Stay here. I'm going to check it out."

"You're not calling for backup?"

Morgan ignored me and withdrew his pistol as he crept around the back of the house. When he was out of sight, I made my move and took off in the opposite direction. From behind, Morgan called out after me to stop. I dipped into an alleyway as his car started.

I only had one advantage over Morgan. I had an address, but he knew the town. I plugged the address into the maps and ran through a maze of alleyways, splashing through puddles of rancid liquid.

214 Franklin Street was much like a handful of the other houses on the street -- boarded and long since abandoned. Parkside, despite its quaint beauty, was a city amidst revitalization. Gentrification had missed this part of town. I took a step toward the house, its gaping front door inviting me.

Morgan's cruiser came to a squealing stop behind me. "Stop!"

Ignoring his command, I opened the front door and tried to step inside. A beam of light cast itself through a crack in a wall, illuminating splatters of blood throughout the house. For the second time in less than fifteen minutes, bile rose to my mouth, and I began to dry heave. Becca had to be in here somewhere. The bastard promised as much.

Behind me, a gun cocked, and I slowly moved my hands upward.

"Turn around slow. Don't do anything stupid."

I did as Morgan commanded. "Detective, you really don't understand—"

"It is *you* who doesn't understand. I've warned you already. You're tampering with evidence and impeding a police investigation."

I replied with a stutter as I floundered around for an explanation, some excuse that would get me out of jail time.

"Take a step back," Morgan said as he holstered his weapon. "What's that you're standing on?"

I looked down to see an envelope beneath my foot and reached for it.

"Stop!" Morgan said. "Take a step back toward me."

I did as I was told. Morgan then snatched up the envelope, pulled out a paper slip, and unfolded it. He studied it, then did an about-face and quickly closed the space between us. He waved a paper in front of me.

"Explain this!" he shouted, shoving the paper aggressively into my face.

I read, then reread the note.

You've got your award-winning story. Now make me infamous.

"I'm going to check things out while you develop a reasonable explanation," Morgan grunted as he skulked away.

Chapter 31

I thought I'd seen it all. I'd seen blood splattered in just about every direction and creative liberties that one crazed mind could concoct. I'd seen people with gunshot wounds, stab injuries, and broken bones. I could stomach just about anything you could throw at me. Years of crime scene investigating had made me numb to just about anything. What amazed me was the tremendous amount of vomit that came from me upon walking into this scene. It was horrific.

I gazed around the room. Hanging like a garland for Christmas was what I believed to be a lower intestine. From wall to wall, individual organs adorned any free space amidst the clutter of damaged photographs and paintings. Hair, skin, and bone stretched about. The floor was coated in a sticky, disgusting slurry of blood and gore. Each squish of my boot sent a slight gag reflex through my body until I couldn't keep composed any further.

"Son of a fuck!" I blurted out as I wiped at my mouth.

I turned to address Jasper. I can't imagine how a person not trained or conditioned to deal with this would handle the exhibit laid out before us.

"Hey, don't come in here," I called out to the doorway, letting Jasper know not to come deeper into the home.

No response. I moved back through the house, toward the front door. If anything, I needed air. Some backup would be appreciated, too. Given the scene, I doubt the killer was hiding in the bedroom closet. This sicko had hightailed and was long gone. As I poked my head back out, basking in the fresh air, I noticed Jasper was also of the same mindset to make himself scarce.

"Goddamnit!" I said as I slammed my forearm against the door-frame.

Jasper, as expected, took off. I glanced over to my car. It was still there, so he didn't manage to steal it. This jackwagon ran off on foot. I'm not sure what got him so spooked, either. His nose was buried in his phone texting his boss, girlfriend, or whoever had his attention, so I didn't think he was paying enough attention to find an opening. After seeing that note, I guess he felt he'd done all he could. My mind raced, trying to draw the connection between Jasper and the killer. The letter was the missing piece.

I called in the scene after I returned to my car. I sat on the hood, taking a moment to collect myself. I could see a trail of bloody foot-prints following me to the curb. These boots were trash once I was done. I'd likely be leaving them curbside when I drove away. I needed to talk to someone. I was alone in my thoughts and feelings, and I hated being in my own headspace. I dialed the only number I figured would pick up at any hour.

"Kurt? Is everything alright?" Zahra's voice greeted me with worry on the other end of the line.

I hesitated for a moment. "Yeah. I'm fine. I'm waiting for dispatch to send some cars to a new site. I wanted to get my mind off of it. Hoping you'd oblige."

I could tell Zahra had a bit of worry in her voice as she moved to a different room. "What is it?"

I shifted slightly on the car hood. "This scene. Everything. It's just, you know, too much," I took a deep breath before continuing. "Also, I lost that reporter."

"What do you mean you lost him? How do you just lose a person?"

"He slipped away while we followed a lead. I'm at the end of that lead. It's bad."

"Kurt, I don't want you doing this again. Don't let this consume you," Zahra said, her voice concerned.

"I'm not. The Crazed Lovers killers, or whatever the press wanted to call them, slipped through. I know I obsessed over that for ages. The case went cold, as if they may have stopped killing. My thought had always been that they'd gotten better. That's bothered me since."

"Yes, it has. I know, sweetie. You're a good man, Kurt. Too good. You worry too much and get obsessive."

She called me sweetie. I was sure it was a slip-up. "I just want to make sure these wackos are off the streets for our children's sake."

"I know, and I appreciate you for doing that. You're not Superman. You're not invincible. You need to be safe, Kurt."

I got to thinking about this killer. He'd have to be nearby. Perhaps he lived in the area. This was a lot of work to complete and then take a road trip. This was a quick jaunt from his home.

"This guy is local, Zahra. I need to get him. I can't let him walk away from this."

"I understand, honey. Hey, by the way, someone wants to say hi."

I heard the phone shuffle a bit before I heard Alisa's voice. "Daddy?"

"Hi, sweetheart! How are you doing?"

"Watching a movie on TV with mommy," Alisa answered.

"Well, you guys get back to your movie. I'll see you sometime this week?" I asked.

"Daddy is visiting this week?" I heard Alisa clearly ask Zahra.

There was a bit of shuffle on the phone.

"Hey, I wanted to say I love you, sweetie," I said, wanting to make sure my kids knew that. I always lived life as if it was my last day.

"I love you too. Stay safe, Kurt," Zahra's voice said before hanging up.

I dropped my phone in between my knees and hung my head. My mind was racing. I barely noticed the two SUVs pull up with officers and forensics. Felicity came toward me.

"How bad is it in there?" she asked.

I just looked up at her. She could still see I was a bit green from unease.

"That bad? I'm not looking forward to walking in there."

I watched as Felicity moved inside. She paused for a moment before entering the home. It didn't take long before coming out for her own sanity. She moved toward me immediately.

"Is this the same guy?" she asked.

"Same guy. Jasper got a note," I said, passing the note off to her gloved hands.

"It's already got my prints and Jaspers. If you find any others, that's our man," I said, realizing how contaminated the scene was. "I need to head out of here. I had a rough day. Two scenes in one day. I need to wrap my head around it to process the report."

"Roger Dodger. I get it, Morgan. I'll call if we find anything other than carnage in the scene."

I got into my car. As promised, I kicked off my boots outside the door, leaving them behind in the rearview mirror as I drove away. I needed to get out of this scene, away from this neighborhood, and head somewhere safe. Somewhere my mind could unwind. My near-empty apartment was just the place that would work. No distractions. Just sleep. I set course for home, ready to crash on the couch as soon as possible.

Chapter 32

I couldn't get the images out of my head. Ropes of tendrils. Dripping blood. A congealed mess. My stomach rejected itself as dry heaves threatened to turn my insides out.

Despite the best efforts of Morgan's large frame, I was still able to glimpse past him at the interior of the home. My eyes wandered to make out the victim. A blonde, short pixie cut, strung up across the foyer. Her hair gently catching the entering breeze, dancing eerily in the evening light.

I'd lost it, and the grotesque profanity haphazardly strung and splashed about the house put me over the edge. Somehow, my limbic system had shut off any sense of empathy for the slain. In my desperate attempts at a groundbreaking scoop and a sick desire to please the Disfigurer, I'd managed to disconnect with humanity by only seeing the women as sensational subjects — the objects of another man's sick pleasure.

It had taken my mind a moment to register the images, then reboot. Then another minute as Morgan disappeared inside, and for my legs to receive the signal it needed.

My body reacted and did the one thing I could think to do in this situation; I ran like hell.

Perhaps I was running from the scene, but that wouldn't be enough. I was running from the sicko, and that sicko was me.

With a friend dead and Becca at the mercy of a psychopath, I needed to do something. The scene at the blood house couldn't have been much different from the scene in the department store. It was clear to me then and made more evident that this guy planned meticulously. How else could he rope out the place with human innards? He was stockpiling women and possibly men. He had no reason to discriminate if he intended to toss about guts and bloodied, dismembered parts, then phone it in hours or maybe days later. He only meant to make it look rushed.

It felt good to run.

Thoughts poured through me in a stream of consciousness, and one dot connected with another. Since Morgan hadn't arrested me, I could only assume Griffin hadn't called the police. And if he had, Morgan already vouched for me but didn't bother to inform me. Not that he was under obligation to do so. Cops did what cops did, and journalists did what journalists did. We both had a knack for operating in the gray areas, especially when it came to getting our story or getting our man.

But in my case, my story and my guy had the upper hand. He had Becca, his Ace of Spades, but he didn't know about me, the wild card. I needed to beat him at his own game.

I don't know how long or where I ran, but I knew I'd arrived when I barged through my motel room door. I was driven by a need to write, but not for the narration. No, I needed to oust this guy. I'd make good on his demand for infamy, but I'd paint him to be the worst kind. Men like Charles Manson and Ted Bundy were shit stains on the sheets of society. Still, people were fascinated with them and even found the ability for empathy, attributing their tortured souls to some past trauma. But my guy, the Disfigurer, he killed, tortured, and mangled for the fun of it. Empathy for the man and some past trauma wouldn't be able to color his persona any other way. This killer was a stain on society that even the Tide-Stick of justice could erase.

No, he needed to be burned.

I pulled my laptop out of my satchel and fired it up. With laser focus, I pounded out a piece that would indirectly explain away my recent email hack. It would detail how I let a psychopath dupe me into an experience of a lifetime, using innocent women as pawns on his chessboard of notoriety.

Keystroke after keystroke, one word stringing with another, forming sentences, each more detailed than the next, consumed me. When I was finished, it was only then that I glimpsed long enough at my surroundings.

The bed was made, and the floor was clear of vomit. And, upon my nightstand sat a box. I knew then the maid had not been here to clean. No, someone else had tampered with my room, and that someone had left me a gift.

I swallowed back dread. My story would certainly oust him as a pleasure-seeking wanna-be who gets off on dismemberment. But what would the box do to me? Surely, he wasn't showing me his hand.

With the care one might use to handle fine China, I picked up the box. It was a simple glossy blue cardboard stamped decoratively with a name: *Kresge*. Someone had taken care to neatly tape it shut, rather than fold over the flaps.

I slid a finger beneath one of the flaps and pulled, ripping the tape, along with some of the glossy blue away from the box. When it had opened, my eyes beheld a severed hand caked with dry blood. The ring finger was decorated with a familiar ring, the one I gave to Becca when I proposed.

I swallowed back bile and forced myself to look closely. While my hippocampus wanted to run in overdrive, I needed to step back and assess before I was paralyzed with emotion.

Something about the hand was off. It wasn't Becca's but belonged to another. I don't know what possessed me to do so, but I touched it and found it wasn't cold and fleshy. No, it was solid to the touch.

The Disfigurer was toying with me. I knew that now, and he knew I'd recognize it as a mannequin's hand. It was a clue, as was the box.

Suddenly, it all came together. He was hiding there all this time, watching and waiting.

I set the box down. Becca had time, and I needed the full force of Parkside Police behind me. I called Detective Morgan. Immediately the phone went to voicemail.

I called again and got the same result. This time I left a message.

"Morgan, when you get this message, call me. I know where the Disfigurer is."

I hung up, then paced back and forth. Then I called again, and again it went to voicemail.

"Fuck it, Morgan. We've missed it the entire time. He's got Becca, and he's hiding out at the old Kresge's. Meet me there. I'm going there with or without you."

Leaving my things in the room, I darted outside, dashing into the motel office, and immediately bombarded the kid with cash.

"That's all I have. Charge the rest to my room, but please let me borrow your car."

The attendee counted it out, frowned, then counted it again. He looked at me and laughed.

"Fuck kind of place you think we're running here, buddy?"

Heat rose to my neck, then to my face.

The attendee handed me back the cash. "Listen, man. Talk to Rob down at Clifton Garage two blocks South. He's got a few beaters he can sell you for this kind of cash."

Ashamed, I mumbled a thanks and shoved the cash back into my pocket.

Minutes later, and out of breath, I found the seedy joint known as Clifton's Garage. A handful of wrecks likely used for spare parts sat out front, and one car was raised up on the lift within the garage. With no one in sight, I headed toward the door to the right of the garage. Concrete and paint chips flaked and crumbled off the building's outside walls, and the door creaked when I entered.

The office reeked of stale oil and gasoline, and the desk was littered with a scattering of papers. I tapped the bell on the desk. When it didn't make a sound, I called out.

"Anyone here?"

A moment passed, and my question was answered when a bone-thin man wearing a ratty oil-stained button-up and matching slacks entered from the same door.

"Saw you come in. You a cop?"

"Reporter," I said. "Do you mind if I show you my credentials?"

He nodded, and I reached in my pocket and showed him my press pass and driver's license. As he examined it, I rambled.

"The attendee up at the motel said you might be able to help me. I need a car and fast. My fiancée, she's—"

"Your business is your business. How much cash you got?"

"I little over three hundred," I said.

He glared at me for a moment, then he went behind the counter and pulled out a notebook. As he thumbed through the pages, I shifted my weight from foot to foot. Every part of me wanted to scream for him to hurry it up, but I had to contain myself. I had to pull it together. Three hundred wasn't much, and this guy could just as easily shoot me or laugh me out of his establishment.

Just as I was about to offer him more cash, he spoke.

"You going far?"

"Fifteen or sixteen miles."

He pulled out a steel cabinet and opened it. "Three hundred even for the Taurus out back."

"I'll take it."

He tossed me the keys. "Burn it when you're done if you're doing anything illegal."

Keys in hand, I ran out back and found the faded blue sedan with rust on the hood. It'll have to do. I climbed into the front seat and keyed the ignition. The engine whined and choked, then, mercifully, it turned over and fired up.

As I drove off, I rang Morgan repeatedly until he answered, or I found myself parked outside Kresge's, right across from where this whole thing started.

{ 33 }

Chapter 33

I was jolted awake by a flurry of messages. I don't even remember falling asleep. I just laid down on the couch, and now the phone was losing its shit. I reached over and grabbed the cell. My eyes hadn't entirely adjusted themselves to being awake, but I could swear I missed about forty texts and half as many missed calls. My email had a dozen unread notifications as well. Every single one was from Jasper. I damn near forgot I tossed him my card. I unlocked my phone and clicked the messages to start this long dissertation that was sent to me. As I clicked the messages, a call came in, my thumb accidentally pressing answer.

"He did it! He friggin did it!" a crazed laugh broke up the muttering. "That son of a bitch did it!"

I barely had time to look at the caller ID, but I knew it was Jasper. "Did what? What happened?"

Jasper let out some frustrated screams. I could hear things slamming against walls or something banging. I couldn't quite make out what was going on in the background.

"Jasper, talk to me," I said calmly.

"The killer, Morgan! The fucking killer! He crossed a line today, bucko! Believe you me, he doesn't want to be on the receiving end of what I'm about to do!"

"Jasper, what is going on? Where are you at?"

"I have an address, Morgan. I sent it to you earlier. I know where he is. He's got Becca!" Jasper stammered out in anger.

"Slow down. Who's Becca?" I asked, genuinely perplexed.

"My fiancée! I thought you knew?" Jasper went into some muttering that I couldn't make out. "It doesn't matter. Doesn't matter at all. Not anymore."

"I'll get some units dispatched to the address. I can come to get you, and we can go together if you'd like?" I asked, trying to diffuse the situation and regain control.

"Don't bother! I'm already here, Morgan. I'm handling it!" Jasper barked as he hung up the phone.

I held the phone to my ear for another moment before realizing the line had gone dead. I knew I had to shuffle through dozens of messages to figure out the address. I quickly moved to the car, face buried in the phone for an address. I was almost to the bottom floor in the elevator before finding which message contained that precious information. I called dispatch immediately.

I put the address into my phone's GPS. I hadn't even processed where it was until I saw it pop up on the map. I knew the location. I went into the trunk, retrieving my flak jacket before heading off to stop Jasper from making a poor decision. I wanted to play it safe. I needed to see my kids tomorrow. Dispatch let me know a QRF team was preparing and will be en route soon. I sped off to make up for the lost time. Every extra second is more time to let Jasper do something stupid. How did we miss it? This guy was good. Who would ever suspect a defunct department store as a headquarters? We just pulled our units off overwatch, too. Slick sonofabitch. He performed his kills in one while leaving the opposing store as a viable hideout to keep an eye on us. They always say to never shit where you eat, but this guy didn't get the memo.

{ 34 }

Chapter 34

The piece of shit junker sputtered and rolled to a stop in the parking lot. When last I was here, the parking lot was naturally empty. But now, nine cars were parked evenly in the lot. They varied in make and model, from sedans to pickup trucks to convertibles. Unlike the car that managed to get me here, these were well-maintained. I didn't have time to speculate on how they got there or whether they were related to the Disfigurer's nefarious plans.

Though it didn't really matter, I popped the Taurus into park and hopped out. Then I ran with the hope that Becca was still alive somewhere inside. She left me once on this trip when the story consumed me. I wouldn't lose her from some psychopath who planned to mangle her body to satisfy his sick fantasies.

I found the custodial door Patti and I used earlier when we revisited the old crime scene. A light flickered overhead, whereas before, we needed flashlights. Either someone had managed to pirate some power, or the Disfigurer made it easier for me to find him in a department store's otherwise dark and abandoned shell.

I passed what was once a food court, then came to an open area with vaulted ceilings. The familiar police tape still marked out the drying crime scene. Patti and I shared a moment of discovery there, and I imagined her and myself ducking once again beneath the tape to survey the blood-stained walls and floors.

A chord of laughter echoed through the building while a sudden draught of moldy air sent chills through my body. Behind me, the hollowed-out department store of an old Kresge beckoned me to enter where I knew doom awaited. Equally, I knew the Disfigurer wouldn't have lured me here if Becca wasn't alive. I'd seen the crime scenes up close. He was slow and meticulous, savoring every detail of the experience. He'd filmed Patti's dismemberment in intimate detail, but that wasn't enough.

This was no longer about his personal pleasure anymore. He needed someone else as his witness to share in his final act. Did he need validation, or was he just tired of being alone? That wasn't clear to me, and I doubted it was clear to him.

I knew he stood poised and ready to strike somewhere in the shadows beyond. Between us lay a maze of empty display shelves and mannequins. I'd play along, then I'd change the rules.

I kept to the right wall as I made my way to the back of the store. No way was I going to let myself be grabbed from behind. Eventually, the store's footprint came to an intersection. Again, I kept to the right as I wasn't willing to risk exposure. In the emptiness beyond, light poured through an open archway. I moved faster, still keeping my back to the wall. My movement sent echoes off the bare walls. I stopped, then slowed. Though the Disfigurer likely knew I was already here, I still needed to be as stealthy as possible.

I found the archway opening to an access hallway which led to another door. When I came to the door, I gritted my teeth and turned the knob slowly. It was unlocked and opened with ease. Entering, I quickly surveyed the room. I didn't have time to examine the nest this guy had created for himself out of newspapers and photographs. No, I had to find Becca, and she wasn't in here. Then I sought out another door. It was shut, and I knew without a doubt that's where he had to be keeping Becca if she was still alive.

I grabbed the knob, twisted it, and pulled the door open without another thought. Though she was tied in the center of the room and her back was to me, I recognized Becca in an instant.

I called out her name and ran and knelt beside her. She was unconscious and tied up. I grabbed the rope and wrestled with the knots, but they wouldn't budge.

Strong hands pulled me away. I screamed as I wrestled with my attacker's grip, but his arm wrapped around my neck. He pulled me into himself, and I could smell his unwashed body. Stale, coppery sweat consumed my senses as I struggled against the man's tightening grip around my neck and chest.

My head swam, and my vision blurred. I awoke to someone violently slapping me on the face, then hoisting me to my feet and placing the sharp edge of a blade on my neck.

The Disfigurer had me in check. So much for changing the rules of the game. He'd been seven moves ahead of me, and I didn't see it coming.

{ **35** }

Chapter 35

The department store was one of the many crime scenes I'd seen all too much in the past few weeks. Two dead anchor stores of a mall were the ideal places to set up camp. Frankly, I was impressed this guy was two steps ahead of us. Most killers are mindless, half-educated idiots who make half-cocked decisions. This guy, The Disfigurer, was a few notches above. He wanted to get caught. Or he intended to lay yet another trap to tie up loose ends. In either case, I notified dispatch to rally units to Kresge's, the adjacent and equally empty store that once was a monument to capitalism.

In the parking lot were several cars. Considering this place wasn't open for business and hadn't been for over a decade, this didn't make sense. Some beater Taurus with scratches all over it, rust almost complimented the off blue paint job, parked haphazardly in front of the store. I had a sinking feeling that it was Jasper. He was a wildcard but highly predictable. He likely stole the vehicle from the roadside or paid some unwitting kid for their first car. I checked my sidearm to be sure I still had a full magazine. I didn't know who or how many people were involved with this. I was short one round, which left me fourteen more. More than plenty before a reload.

I gently shut my car door so as not to alert anyone to my presence. I figured it was all in vain, considering this asshole likely knew my moves and was expecting me here. Something was unsettling about the giant glass windows still full of dilapidated mannequins as I approached. As if mocking the previous scene, they were staged in lifelike poses, fully intact. I tried the door handle, which moved with ease. I pulled the door open wide and slipped into the building. The air was stale, smelling of mold. One thing this place didn't reek of was death, and that was reassuring that I was still on time.

Ahead of the entryway, one light illuminated from the rear, from what used to be the women's lingerie department, if memory serves. I'd taken Zahra to Kresge's so many times in the past. I'd have to wander the store to find where she was hiding, which oftentimes led me to that corner of the store. I moved forward, weapon drawn and at the ready. Memories of pushing a stroller with Davey in it fluttered back into my mind. We really did like this place. All of this online shopping likely killed these places. It's what happens when you can't keep up with the times, I suppose.

The light poured from a service hallway. I'd never noticed it before, but then again, who's really looking for service exits while shopping for a new pair of slacks. I pushed the door fully open. The hallway was long, consisting of security rooms, management offices, and a warehouse loading area. The sign to the right of me as I entered detailed everything I'd encounter. What it didn't describe was which one of these rooms the killer had taken up residence. Every wasted second was another moment I could spend stopping this sicko. I looked at the crudely designed map and tried to decide where Jasper, the killer, and Jasper's lady were. Time was not on my side at all. I couldn't wait for backup. I glanced back at the map, decided, and moved for the room.

I counted the large doors as I passed them. One on my left, one on my right, followed by another on the left. The last on the right seemed the ideal room to me. There was a loading bay the killer could easily escape, and it was the only room with a second floor. It was the most likely, and most confusing room to toy with me in. For a demented mind, it was the ideal playground. I took a deep breath, moving into the room.

The door creaked with a minor squeal. It was more than enough to give my position up, however. It didn't matter. The killer knew I was here. Every light in the warehouse flipped on with an aggressive buzz. My eyes took a moment to adjust to the light. This would have been the ideal time to get the jump on me, but he waited. Why did he wait? Why was everything a game with this asshole? I let my eyes adjust to the new lighting and scanned the room. I could only see a set of iron stairs to my right, leading to a small foreman's office-type room. The windows were covered, likely with newspaper, to keep me from looking in. I'd have taken a shot at the guy if I could see him.

Creeping slowly up the stairs, each footstep seemed to give me away. My boot landed with an audible thud that seemed to echo throughout the entire warehouse. I felt like a damn T-Rex stomping through some defunct genetic engineering park after some kids. I reached the top of the landing, leading me to a door several feet from the top step. I moved in, sticking to the right side in the event he took a shot through the door. As I approached, I heard shuffling inside. Readying my gun, I grabbed the knob and thrust the door open.

Inside, I found the inner workings of a madman. Newspapers tacked onto the windows to block out light outside. On the walls; photographs, drawings, and more littered the off-white painted cinderblock. Ahead of me, the coup de gras, the killer. His arm wrapped around Jasper's neck, the other arm wielding a small hunting knife. I could tell the blade was sharp. Based on the curvature, I could tell it was a bone knife. More than enough to slit Jasper's throat.

"You don't have to do this," I said calmly to the killer, never deviating my aim from his direction.

"The dolls are all burned now, aren't they?" said the killer.

I don't know if it was the demeanor in which he said it or *what* he said, but it was unsettling. I figured I could stall for time and let backup assist.

"What dolls? Who's burned?" I asked, playing dumb as much as I could in an attempt to get him talking.

"The dolls, Detective Morgan. The dolls. I planned to add more dolls to my shelf this week," the killer said, gesturing to a shelf in the corner of the room. "More dolls. More fire from the Gods."

Christ, was this guy referring to his victims as "dolls"? Was the "fire" his chemical for melting the parts down? I really didn't know what his angle was in all of this. It never hurts to ask, right?

"Why are you making the dolls, uh," I fished for him to give me a name.

"Call me, Daniel. Yes, I like that."

"Okay, Daniel, why the dolls?" I asked, playing the game.

"Dolls last forever. See their pictures? Forever!" Daniel said.

I could tell I was dealing with someone wholly unhinged and disconnected from society. I needed to find an opening and ask more questions. "And the latest doll?"

"Oh, that is a beautiful doll, indeed. Very breakable, however. Not durable at all. Broken inside and out, yes," Daniel said as he slowly loosed his grip on Jasper.

I made eye contact with Jasper. His mouth gagged; he couldn't do anything but the same grunts and groans he'd been making, so he had no chance of giving my idea away. I'd seen it in movies and television but had no idea how successful this idea would work. Once I saw red liquid begin to flow from Jasper's throat, I decided it was now or never. I squeezed the trigger, firing a round directly into Jasper's shoulder, striking the killer as well.

Jasper screamed in pain through his gag, dropping to the floor. I saw my chance and put one more into the killer's leg, dropping him to the ground. He quickly dropped the bone knife from his hands. Keeping the barrel trained on Daniel, I moved forward to kick the knife away from him. I needed to cuff him, but I didn't want to be the only one able to subdue him. I figured I could keep him talking. He barely reacted to being shot. I guess Jasper did all of the reacting for him.

"Where's the girl, asshole?" I demanded.

Daniel looked up at me for a moment, smiling through a blood-coated face. Some of Jasper's blood spurted onto him after the shot.

"Daniel, goddamnit! What's the point of this?" I barked, adjusting my stance over him.

"Point? Do I need one? I wanted to make the dolls. They weren't perfect before, but now they are. Can't you see that? They'll never sin again. They'll never cheat again. They'll never lie again."

Daniel was insane. "Is that what you think? You took their free will away, man! That's not cool." I was at a loss for words. I didn't know what to tell him. I just needed more time for the backup to arrive. "Why burn the body in the chemical if you want them to stay perfect?"

Daniel barely looked at me. He looked like he was miles away, possibly trying to figure out that part of the equation himself. Crazy never makes sense, and he is living proof. I cuffed him to the table, returning to Jasper, who was moaning through his gag on the floor. I removed the tape from across his mouth, which caused him to shriek even louder than ever.

"You fucking shot me!"

"Relax, Jasper. It's not our first rodeo," I said, dismissing his complaint. "You should be used to it by now."

Jasper glanced over at his shoulder. I damn near lined up the shot to strike the flesh of the previous wound. You could see where the gauze and bandages were practically torn away by the bullet. His eyes made contact with the wound, which didn't help his complaining. I looked around and saw some newspapers still stacked on the table. I padded his shoulder as best as I could. I had to check out the other rooms and the steel door across the catwalk area.

I double-checked that Daniel was down on the ground. He wasn't going to be much of a problem. A younger guy, probably mid-thirties. He was clearly following in the other killer's footsteps. He'd have started in the womb if he was one of the nutjobs I'd been tracking all those years ago. I'd love to be a fly on the wall of his psych eval. I bet it's the cliche mommy issues and torturing animals. I shook the thoughts out of my head as I approached the door. This is where I'd keep a victim if I were Daniel. This is where Jasper's lady is, or at least, was. I gripped my pistol as my free hand opened the door.

Light spilled into the cold, empty room. There, inside, I saw what was to be a horrific scene to unfold and stopped early. Likely Jasper's interference bought the time needed. A large drum full of the chemical compound and a wooden chair containing a person in the room. Becca, I assumed. There was blood around her. I moved in to see if it was hers or a previous victim. As I drew closer, she wasn't moving. Slowly, I holstered my sidearm and placed my hand on her shoulder. She shrieked like a banshee.

"Calm down. I'm Detective Morgan. I'm here to help," I tried to say as calmly and reassuringly as possible. "Can you tell me your name?"

The young girl flailed a bit in the chair. She was restrained. I wanted to remove the restraints, but I also didn't want her to injure herself.

"I'm going to let you out of here, ok? Please stay calm."

I reached for the buckle that strapped her in. It released with a soft click, forcing her body to slump forward. As I hit the following two clips, it became clear who's blood this was.

"We're going to get you medical attention, ok?" I said, trying to keep my composure.

Just before the distal radius, cutting into the forearm, I could see she was missing her hand. I quickly pulled my phone out to radio in additional support. The killer sealed off the wound, but it was a sloppy job. I don't think he meant to leave her like this. I think he was savoring the moment, taking it piece by piece. This son of a bitch was meticulously cutting. It was sloppy yet artistic. I wrapped her wrist in my overshirt. I didn't know what else to do, and my button-down seemed to be the best contribution to the madness.

Once I'd managed to calm her down, I escorted her out to join Jasper. He was hysterical at his own wound to notice I'd placed his lady down nearby. She was mostly in shock herself. I took a moment to just slump against the wall and relax. The killer, still restrained, grumbled and moaned in pain. Daniel would live. I reached for my chest pocket for my cigarettes, clutching nothing but my white undershirt. I gave my shirt away. I lacked the energy or drive to retrieve them, so I slowly closed my eyes to collect myself amidst the chaos.

My rest was disturbed by the gentle sounds of several dozen tactical boots, screamed orders, and doors being thrust open. The calvary was here. Once the first officer burst through the threshold, I pointed toward Daniel, whom they immediately surrounded. The EMTs were second on the scene, quickly dropping to the ground with various first aid items. Jasper and Becca were being cared for immediately. One EMT had the unfortunate pleasure of patching up that psychopath. In my report, I'd have to explain why several rounds were discharged, with two of them being in Jasper. That was future Kurt's problem. Right now, I wanted to bask in the silence. I got my man. There's no greater feeling, I believe, than that. And you can quote me on that one.

The End

Epilogue

In the months following the capture of the killer named Daniel, quite a bit happened. I was hailed as a hero back at the station. I can't begin to say how encouraging it is to hear them call me Detective Sergeant Kurtis Morgan once more. Closure on this case offered a bit of relief, but would never quite remove the disappointment and disgrace that came with losing a partner and cold casing one of my top targets. It did, however, help in some ways.

Zahra and I have been working on our relationship. With being clean and sober for nearly six months at this point, I feel like a new man. Davey began a fasttrack IT program with his school, which has been over my head in more ways than I can dream up. Alisa has just been growing up so fast. We've got tickets as a family to enjoy a local broadway tour of, you guessed it: Frozen the Musical. I cannot go on about how excited I am for this performance. If you thought the animated songs were great, be ready for the live versions.

Felicity got married to her high school sweetheart. We attended the wedding, greeted by a breakfast buffet and Celtic musical group at the reception. Dwayne, well, he's still Dwayne. Looking for love in the wrong places, to include at the wedding. Felicity gave him a scolding once she returned from the honeymoon, livid about his intentions to seduce the groomsman. Can't blame a guy for trying, right?

I half expected, after our interactions, to receive an invitation to the Marks wedding. We kept in touch loosely in the following months from the case, but grew distant as time progressed. I had my hands full coaching a little league team, running a homicide team, and balancing anything else life would throw at me. As it turned out, Jasper was never able to write the article of his dreams. Becca, his fiancée, apparently left him not long after their return home.

Jasper told me he had no energy or effort to finish his award-winning story based on his account. Writing about Becca hurt every inch of his fiber as he typed the words in his word processor. I offered to help him tell the story. I felt it was a kind gesture, as I'd be able to fill in any blanks in his tale. A week later, my inbox was filled with research, photos, notes, and completed manuscript page drafts. After that, I hadn't heard from Jasper Marks.

I phoned his publication headquarters, the Daily Sentry. The lovely woman on the phone let me know that Jasper covers sports for the paper, primarily racing. I felt bad for him, but hoped for the best all the same.

Daniel the killer, as it turns out, was exactly as Jasper pegged in his article. Considering he was throwing darts at a million possibilities, he hit a bullseye with one. Daniel Krueger, age 31, was in a long term relationship with fellow college student Amy White. Amy, as you may have guessed, was a 28 year old blonde. We ran leads on her, finding that she'd been missing for years. Her sister had suspicions of him since she went missing, but nothing ever flagged him.

As part of a plea deal with the courts, Daniel walked us to the site that Amy was located. We dug up a mostly decomposed body, dismembered, and haphazardly dumped in a shallow grave. He had the decency to at least cover her with some dirt to keep the wildlife off her. Forensics ran some tests, finding traces of various household chemicals. Faint as they were, it was enough to determine they were some of the key ingredients found in his perfected vat of liquid.

It's amazing what people will do for love, or lack thereof. The mind is a complicated catacomb of emotions, ebbing and flowing with day to day activities. Love is the driving force that keeps everyone pushing forward. Whether it is love of family, children, work, or hobby, we push forward daily, striving to improve the relationship every step of the way. When something comes along that impedes our progress, some regroup and resurface with a newfound passion. Others, dismember their loved ones, leaving them pisspoorly buried, covered in chemical burns.

About the Authors

Harry Carpenter

Harry Carpenter, writer of "Tales from an Ex-Husband" and the "Fubar" series, is a fan of horror, science fiction, and suspense. Born in Baltimore, Maryland, a city full of illustrious authors and performers, Harry began writing in elementary school. He formally pursued his passion, releasing his first book "Tales From An Ex-Husband" in 2019.

Harry has since won the "Best Short Short Story" award twice in the Veteran's Administration writing contest and was featured as the bestselling author in local bookstores.

Using his experiences in the United States Army, various retail and fast food establishments, childhood encounters, and chaotic first marriage, he has developed a mind for creativity.

He is a huge fan of cats, video games, and quirky science fiction and horror movies. He also films an internet web series called "The Web-Pool" on YouTube, as well as volunteers with the "Charm City Ghostbusters," a charity organization out of Baltimore who, as the name dictates, dress as the Ghostbusters 1984 movie.

Harry now lives in Baltimore with his wife and cats.

More information can be found at www.hcarpenterwriter.com

About Timothy R. Baldwin

Tim grew up in Syracuse, New York. He currently resides in Maryland, where he teaches English, Creative Writing, Film, and Theatre at the middle school level. At the insistence of his students, he began writing seriously in 2014. He credits his love for stories to his mother, who spent countless hours reading to him and his siblings growing up. Growing up, he devoured the literary works of C.S. Lewis, J.R.R. Tolkien, Piers Anthony, and many others. Mysteries, thrillers, and fantasies are among the genres he most frequently reads. When he's not writing, he's reading, teaching, camping, or at a live music concert.

For more great stories by Timothy R. Baldwin, join his mailing list
https://dl.bookfunnel.com/hwccadt2eh
or visit https://www.indiesunited.net/timothy-baldwin

Other Works by the Authors

Timothy R. Baldwin
The Kahale and Claude Mystery Series
   -Camp Lenape
   -Shadows of Doubt
   -Operation Varsity Blues
   -A Bazaar Christmas
A Shot at Mercy
A Crock of Sundries

Harry Carpenter
The Fubar Series
   -Blackout
   -Out of Element
Spooky Tales and Scary Things
Spooky Tales and Scary Things 2
Memoirs of a Crazed Mind